W9-CBC-252

CHASE BRANCH LIBRARY
17731 W. SEVEN MILE RD.
DETROIT, MI 48235
578-8002

FEB 08

CH

LIZARD PEOPLE

Also by Charlie Price

Dead Connection

CHARLIE PRICE

LIZARD

PEOPLE

A Deborah Brodie Book
Roaring Brook Press
New York

Text copyright © 2007 by Charlie Price

A Deborah Brodie Book
Published by Roaring Brook Press
Roaring Brook Press is a division of Holtzbrinck Publishing
Holdings Limited Partnership
175 Fifth Avenue, New York, New York, 10010

www.roaringbrookpress.com

All rights reserved
Distributed in Canada by H. B. Fenn and Company, Ltd.

Library of Congress Cataloging-in-Publication Data

Price, Charlie.
Lizard people / Charlie Price. — 1st ed.
p. cm.
"A Deborah Brodie book."
Summary: While visiting his mentally ill mother at a psychiatric
hospital, high school junior Ben Mander starts talking to a young
man who claims that he travels back and forth between the
present and the year 4000, searching for a cure for mental illness.
ISBN-13: 978-1-59643-190-4
ISBN-10: 1-59643-190-3
[1. Mental illness—Fiction. 2. Family problems—Fiction.] I. Title.
PZ7.P92477Li 2007
[Fic]—dc22
2007002168

1 2 3 4 5 6 7 8 9 10

Roaring Brook Press books are available for special promotions
and premiums. For details, contact: Director of Special Markets,
Holtzbrinck Publishers.

Book design by Angela Carlino
Printed in the United States of America
First edition September 2007

To my daughter, Jessica Rose, with love:

Once I cradled you against my chest in one hand and
smoothed your hair with the other.
Now I cradle you against my heart and smooth your hair
in my dreams.
—from *Rose*, a poem by Charlie Price

ACKNOWLEDGMENTS

I am thankful to have Deborah Brodie as my editor. Collaborating with her is like singing harmony. I treasure her compassion, her wisdom. I am very glad that she embraced *Lizard People*.

I am similarly fortunate to have wonderful agents, Tracey and Josh Adams, and I continue to appreciate their professional acumen and their unflagging efforts on my behalf. Further, I respect Ms. Lauren Wohl for the many great ideas she brings to my literary projects.

This book could not and would not have been written without the daily encouragement and readership of my darling wife, Joan Pechanec, who, time and again, put aside her own agenda and read the latest chapter to tell me what worked and what clanked.

My book writing would not have begun without the inspiration and friendship of Chris Crutcher. I appreciate his graciousness and humor.

I also thank Mr. Bill Siemer, who challenges me to better understand story-craft on a weekly basis over corned beef and eggs.

I am grateful to Celeste White for her expertise, and I am in debt to several friends and readers for their support and straight feedback. I will simply list them in thanks: George Rogers, Kit Anderton, Melinda Brown, Dr. Burley Packwood, and Kate Anderton.

I have benefited from canny technical advice on a variety of matters. I heartily thank Dr. Steve Hudgens, Physicist; Lucy Rogers, RN, BSN; Jay Roitman, DO, Medical Director, Hill Country Community Clinic; Mr. George Wolf, Biologist; and Mr. Manuel Garcia, Attorney.

—C. P.

Not the Police

I'm driving too fast. The last thing I need right now is to get stopped by the police. A traffic officer might know I knew Marco. They could think I helped him escape. There might be a warrant out for this car. I don't think so, but anything's possible. They might know all about Mom and even believe I'm crazy, too.

I don't know why I'm so revved up. I'm not afraid. Am I? This is just so important! I want people to understand that, want them to know what I know. I have to get to the Ludlows and tell them this story.

I guess I'm a little overexcited, but you can't keep a

secret like this. Not something that will actually change the world. Make thousands of people well. Turn science on its nose. I mean, it's not like I have the answers, but I know the direction to go in. I'm the only one who really knew Marco.

Z will help me get a grip. She'll listen to me and figure out what to do next. She's Hubie's sister. Sophomore in college. Three years older than I am. Smart and funny and quirky and so different! If she isn't home? What is today? What *is* today? Even Hubie could help. He's practically a scientist already. Or Mrs. Ludlow. She'll know what to do. But not the police. Not right now. I'm not ready.

You can't give a story like this to just anybody.

A Month Ago

I could see Mom with a death grip on one of the secretary's heads. It looked like Mrs. Vance, our across-the-street neighbor. The principal had one hand around Mom's waist, his other hand on her forearm, and he was trying to pull her off the terrified woman. I could see office assistants huddling behind the counter, and two school counselors running through the rear door into the office from the courtyard. Our vice principal, Mrs. Onabi, was on the phone.

I crashed through the office door and tackled Mom, bringing everybody in that tangle to the floor. I was yelling, but Mom was maniacal. She had Mrs. Vance's mouth pulled partway open and was trying to see down inside. The counselors joined the pile, and in a few seconds, the four of us had Mom detached.

"Look at her! Look at her!" Mom was yelling.

"What, Mom?" I was holding her head and one shoulder and whispering in her ear, trying to calm her. "What?" I asked again. "It's me, Ben. What's the matter?"

Mom looked at me for the first time. Her eyes were bloodshot, pupils black whirlpools in a fiery sea of madness. "She—won't—admit—it!" Mom puffed, struggling for breath.

The office was suddenly quiet, except for Mrs. Vance softly sobbing, now behind the counter like a barricade.

We released Mom and stood as she stood. She extended her left arm straight in front of her, pointing, index finger tipped with a long scarlet fingernail. Right at Mrs. Vance. "She," Mom said in a theatrical voice dripping with contempt, "is a Lizard!"

The room was once again silent and stayed that way, practically unmoving, until the police arrived.

Marco

You meet the nicest people in the lobby of a psychiatric hospital. Unless they're drunk or tweaking. Most people are sad and empathetic and easy to approach after what they have just been through with their dad or mom or son or daughter or husband or wife.

I was sitting at the end of a row of connected metal chairs. Two empty seats down from me there was this good-looking blondish guy with short, thick hair, the kind that pretty much always looks right, whether or not it's combed. I think what held my attention was his eyebrows, really bushy and much darker than the rest of his hair. He looked eighteen or nineteen, but something about him seemed even older. He was concentrating, studying what looked like a map of our county. He would think for a few minutes, make a note on a clipboard, and then do the same thing again.

He was pretty much my size, maybe shorter by an inch or so. Face and arms tanned like he was outside a lot. He didn't have the muscle definition of a jock, but he looked in good shape. His clothes were the kind you might buy in an outdoor store, fleece vest, woven cotton shirt, canvas pants, running sandals. I figured this guy had some relative being admitted, too, but he didn't seem nervous, wasn't trying to pretend he was cool. It looked to me like he was just thinking.

I guess I got absorbed watching him, and he noticed.

"Hey," he said, "I'm Marco. How about you?"

"Ben," I said.

"Got somebody here?" he asked, sticking his pen in the metal top of the clipboard.

"My mom," I said. "She's been losing it more often since Dad walked out. Doc thinks it's something like schizo-affective disorder." Was I talking too much?

"Yeah," he said, "my mom's bipolar. I'm just waiting for them to finish with her admission process."

"Bipolar?"

"Yeah, mood swings, depressed to manic. She's had it for a long time. It flares up and really sends her out there. She stops sleeping, starts drinking, has all these amazing projects going that she's talking about all the time. Usually nobody can slow her down until she goes off the deep end and winds up here or in jail."

I was nodding. "My mom's a little like that. She gets off her meds and gets wild and scared and crazy. Nobody can talk her out of it. Your mom work?"

Marco moved a seat closer so it was easier to talk. "She's a decorator, houses and stuff," he said. "She's real intelligent and a good mom when she's down to earth. But every so often, she stops taking her lithium, and then *ho, baby,* watch out! This time she was trying to build a two-story gazebo in the vacant lot across from the post office at 3 A.M. She says she's going to use it as a demonstrator model for her new exterior design package. *Huh-uh.* The police arrested her and brought her here to get medicated."

A woman stuck her head out of the locked unit door. "Next?" she said.

Marco said good-bye and went inside before I thought to get his phone number or his school or anything.

Lizards Hate Red

Trying to take care of Mom after Dad left has played hell with my junior year. I'd missed a fair amount of school, dropped out of wrestling, and resigned as president of the Fly Fishing Club. My teachers and my principal understand what I'm dealing with at home. Especially after today, I bet.

I'm ashamed to admit it, but I was not thinking about Mom as I sat in the hospital admitting area. I was thinking no girl will *ever* go out with me again. It was bad enough before, but now, there'll be a neon sign on my back: WARNING! SANITY-FREE ZONE! No, cancel that.

Most girls will feel sorry for me and that will be even worse. Pity and whispers.

I'm an okay guy. Almost six feet tall, and I usually made the weight and wrestled in the hundred-and-sixty-pound division. I keep my hair short for two reasons: Makes me feel like a wrestler, and my fishing hat fits better and doesn't blow off in the wind. I used to have a bunch of friends. In grade school, middle school, early in high school, in sports, and in summer recreation leagues. This last year most of them have sort of disappeared. They're not mean. I think they're just scared. Like being crazy could be infectious. It is definitely uncool.

I had a couple of girlfriends but I lost them both. I probably know why. For one thing, I was nervous being close to a girl. I watched shows like *Real World* on MTV whenever I got a chance, and tried to understand what girls were like. Did they want to be treated special, doors held and stuff, or was that insulting? Did they want compliments or did they think that compliments were just the way a guy hit on them?

How the hell was I going to keep taking care of Mom? The whole Lizard thing started when Dad left Mom. Left home actually. I don't think they're divorced. I'm pretty sure it was another woman who caused it. I've seen him around town a couple of different times with the same woman. Or maybe, more likely I guess, living with Mom drove him away. I'll probably never know. He won't talk about that when he calls. He gave me his cell phone number but not his address. He always asks me if I need money for sports or dating or anything, and says, if he has to, he'll visit Mom in the hospital. But he won't come by the house. He hasn't been home for three months, since he walked out.

Mom's breakdowns had been happening on and off over the last several years. She had been in some psychiatric hospitals. Here in Riverton, when they had room, down to Sacramento when they didn't. None of the medications, and they had probably given her at least ten by now, seemed to hold her for long. Or maybe some of them worked and she stopped taking them as soon as she came to her senses.

This is the second time I have seen her paint her face with red lipstick. Mom believes that Lizards hate red. She also believes that you can identify a Lizard Person only by looking deep inside his or her mouth and seeing where the human costume ends and the actual Lizard begins.

I don't mean that Dad made Mom go off her rocker. She was that way before. Sometimes she got so lethargic she couldn't even get out of bed for a week. Sometimes she thought that TV shows were talking about her. But the red on the face and the Lizard thing is a recent development.

Dad said there used to be long-term hospitals that would help a person like Mom, but they got closed, so there's nothing like that now.

I'm going to make Dad come back and deal with this.

In the Ozone Layer

When Mom got released and came home a couple of days later, I left school early and was there to meet her. She looked snowed.

"New medication?" I asked.

"Yeah," Mom said. "I'm sleepy. I'm going to bed."

"Want anything to eat? I could fix you something. Tuna sandwich? Can of soup? Cereal with banana in it?"

She didn't respond. Just slogged past me into her bedroom and closed the door.

I wondered if this time she was going to do what the doctor told her. The professionals always said the same thing. Take your medication as prescribed. Keep a regular daily routine.

Last fall Dr. Bhuspodi told Dad and me that Mom's chances to live a normal life again were very slim. The doctor said that there was almost nothing anyone could do but help her feel safe and cared for and hope that the meds would keep her calm and oriented. They were developing new and better psychotropic medications every day, and before too long, they would probably find one that would stop the voices without so many side effects. For now, ideally, she should be in a highly structured rehabilitation home, but the best one was ninety miles from here, in Chico, and it was very expensive, with a mile-long waiting list.

When Mom's on a tear, I mean, like, all paranoid, she is energetic and talkative and full of ideas. When she is medicated, she is usually quiet, embarrassed by what she did when she was psychotic. I know how much guts it takes for Mom to make it through the bad days when she is trying to cope. I see what a hard life it is. I love her so much. But I'm starting to hate her, too. Why can't she get it together and be like other moms? I know it's an illness, but I'm fed up with it!

And there's another tough thing. Mental illness often runs in families. I could get it. I could already have it. In my blood. In my body. In my brain.

Sometimes when Mom is gone, locked in the hospital, I go into her bedroom. I stand in front of her dresser and look at myself in the mirror. I'm embarrassed to say that sometimes I've opened the drawers, picked up one of her slips. So silky. I've sorted through her jewelry. I don't know what I'm looking for. Something of her, maybe, that isn't ruined by the madness. I smell her brush for a quick scent of her hair. I handle the figurines she keeps on her bookcase. I feel close to her in a way I can't seem to anymore when she's present.

I am looking for clues. What happened? What happened to the girl who went to high school and twirled a baton and sang in the choir and rode in convertibles? How did this illness claim her so completely?

Mom keeps her pictures in an old-fashioned striped suitcase under her bed. In my favorite snapshot, she is sitting beside my dad on the porch of a house I don't remember. He's wearing a T-shirt with the sleeves rolled up way too high, his hair longer and shaggy. He has his arm around her and he slouches in a relaxed way that makes it seem like he has already been there for hours and may not move for several more. She's smiling and leaning into his arm. I have taken that picture and put it in my room, in the top drawer of my own dresser, so I can see it whenever I want to.

The range of pictures astounds me: Mom with girl-friends, Mom with groups at football games, Mom in a line waiting to get on a Ferris wheel. Mom with her hair in rollers, dancing with ten or fifteen girls in some gym. She's not like that anymore.

She spends most of her time in her room. She sleeps a lot. She often sits in her rocker and looks out the window at the backyard. This fall I put up a bird feeder by her window, but she hasn't mentioned it and I don't know if it makes any difference. She has all these books but she hardly ever reads.

I had started my homework but I couldn't concentrate. I thought about getting high and going to bed. Recreation for the Mander family? Get sedated and go to sleep. What a life. There was no one to call except my best friend, Hubie, and he was probably still at his after-school job at the Computer Exchange. I wished I had gotten Marco's number. I wanted to ask him if any kind of reasoning ever convinced his mom to take better care of herself.

I got my basketball and went to the neighborhood park to shoot around. I missed my first ten shots and threw my basketball as hard as I could into the street. A landscape company pickup pulling a trailer filled with lawnmowers hit my ball on the first bounce and knocked it way down the street. It made it to the north-south thoroughfare and was flattened by a city bus. *Happy now?*

So I started walking, didn't care where, trying to think my way out of this mess. Without really noticing it, I made it to Hubie's house in time for dinner.

Hubie's mom is a nursing supervisor at our biggest local hospital, but her main role is the neighborhood caretaker. She often has a stray kid at the dinner table. *Hmmm.* She's short and compact, a dynamo. At dinner, she's cooking, bringing more food or more milk, rarely sitting in her chair for more than a minute.

She always, always makes me feel welcome. She asks about my family and listens, but it never feels like prying.

Hubie's dad moves slow, talks slow, and eats slow. He's also short, but unlike his wife, he has a big belly. A book about Emiliano Zapata was at his elbow as he ate.

Hubie has his mom's energy. He was talking nonstop about the idea that communities could begin to provide wireless Internet as part of their infrastructure, like roads and sidewalks. Financed by taxes. He continued talking right through our dessert of vanilla ice cream over white cake with canned peaches.

Where was Z? Was she boycotting family dinners? Hubie's older sister, Kaitlin, would answer only to "Z." She is the bump in the Ludlow family road. Or, maybe in her case, pothole. When Mr. Ludlow asked her what "Z" stood for, she said, "Hypocrisy." When he pointed out there was no z in hypocrisy, she said, "Exactly!"

In the almost-perfect Ludlow family, she is the anti-daughter. She's against everything her mother stands for. She shrivels you with a scathing look if you call her a goth. But what is she? Her ears are like chain-link fences, she has a diamond stud in her nose, and I don't know if it stops there. She favors light makeup and dark eye shadow and thrift-store-chic outfits. Punk diva goes Hindu.

Z has beaucoup causes that she constantly champions: alternatives to fossil fuel, preserve our redwoods, conserve water, feed the hungry, medical care for everyone. And a number of things she argues against: bigotry, war, corporate greed, and so on. I have loved her since the day

15

Hubie and I became friends and he invited me home. She was doing her homework in their living room while she danced to something on MTV. I was in fifth grade and she was in middle school. Now, she's a sophomore at Sierra Junior College in town.

Z was a hurdler in high school until something happened between her and the coach. After that, no more organized sports. Today when she walked into the dining room, she had on black tights under a sari thing, with a ratty jean jacket vest over it. Black knit watchcap on top. A thick book tucked under her arm. "You're not a duck," she said when she saw me. Was that a compliment?

She picked two plums out of the fruit bowl in the middle of the table, took a chicken leg off my plate, and left the room. Hubie's mom rolled her eyes. Mr. Ludlow didn't seem to notice.

Even with the odd moment, it was a comfort to sit and eat with a real family and listen to their conversation and not have to think about anything or do anything. Until afterward, when I bussed the dishes and washed them while Hubie stuck the cleaned ones in the drainer.

"How are things?" he asked, while we were standing together at the sink.

I shook my head. "Not so good," I said, "and I'm pretty sure they're . . ." I stopped myself. I didn't need that kind of prophecy.

I went looking for Z before I headed back home. She was in her room with the door closed. I knocked.

"Closed for a reason," she said.

"Yeah, I figured," I said through the door. "I just thought I'd say hi before I left."

I could hear her move across the floor. It sounded like she sat down and leaned against the door on her side. I sat and leaned, too. Now we were back-to-back with the door between. Was this as close as we'd ever be?

"So, WWF, how's things?" she asked.

World Wrestling Federation. She had come with Hubie to see a couple of my matches last year. In general, she thought wrestling for sport was beyond ridiculous.

"Not so good. Mom blew out at school today. Tackled an office worker. Called her a Lizard."

"Right at school?"

"Big time."

"Pretty tough," she said. "Maybe you should send the office woman a card. Like, uh, 'Sorry we mistook you for a reptile, get well soon, the Manders.' Smooth things over."

"Thanks. You're really helpful."

"Want me to open the door?"

I did. I wanted her to hug me. I wanted to smell that weird oil she puts on and hear the soft jangle of her earrings.

"No," I said. "Why aren't I a duck?"

"Wittgenstein," she said. "The book I'm reading. Philosophy. The clarity of language. You're not a duck, are you?"

"No," I said. Many of my conversations with Z were like this. In the ozone layer. "You okay?"

"Breathing," she said. "Hey, don't let the setbacks get

you down. Life expectancy in Zimbabwe? Thirty-seven. Thousands of kids dying of AIDS every morning. Puts our day-to-day shit in perspective."

I could hear her getting up.

"Later, Head-in-the-Armpit Boy."

I should never have invited her to see me wrestle.

Out to Get You

During the next couple of weeks, I went to school every day, but I couldn't keep my mind on my classes. I kicked myself for not getting Marco's phone number. I would like to have heard how he dealt with his mom's repeated crashes.

A couple of afternoons I went fishing just south of the Cypress Bridge. I worked the flats where some trout were feeding on tiny midges. I caught a couple on those and later, a couple more on yarn salmon eggs. Most of the time, I couldn't tell you what I was thinking about. I was pretty much in another dimension, on automatic pilot, doing what I was told and going wherever I was supposed to be. Other kids kept their distance.

Early on a Tuesday morning, I found out where my mind had been. Hatching a contingency plan.

I was awakened by Mom's keening. I lurched out of bed and found her in the living room, just finishing stuffing red crepe paper all around the edge of the front door. She turned as I came in. She had the red line of lipstick across her forehead and the area from her bottom lip to her chin was solid red.

"Go lock the back door and check the food," she said, digging in the tote bag at her feet.

I knew she was looking for the red metal Celtic cross.

"Mom—"

"Go," she said, not looking up. "They're already here, all over outside. See how much food we have. Make a list."

There was no point in arguing with Mom, paranoid and energized.

I walked into the kitchen, picked up a pad and pencil from the table near the phone, and started: *milk, bacon, lettuce,* just a one-word kind of list. I made a quick inventory of the fridge and pantry, went back into the living room, and handed it to Mom. She was busy tying red ribbons on all the lamps.

The Lizard People were back.

Time for my plan. I grabbed the phone out of the hall and took it to my room.

The woman who answered Dad's cell phone didn't

know where he was. She said maybe he was working out of town. And then she started crying. She said he left one night about two weeks ago and she hadn't seen him since.

"You're his son, right?"

"Yeah."

"If you see him," she said, "ask him to give Charlene, me, a call. I need some help with the rent and we can still be friends. Tell him that. Okay?"

"Did he take any clothes? Or his laptop or anything?"

"No. Not even this phone. We were arguing. He just walked out. Well, his computer was probably still in his car." She coughed. "Hey, you tell him I'm sorry for my part in it. Okay?" she said, sniffling.

"Any idea where he might have gone?" I was picturing what Dad's car looked like.

"Huh-uh. I called the places we go out to. They say they haven't seen him. I called his office, and they say he hasn't been back to work. I even called the police and hospitals this week. I thought maybe something happened to him. They never heard of him."

From the way she pronounced her words, it sounded to me like maybe she had been drinking. Was Charlene such a big improvement over Mom? What is it with Dad?

"I told him he ought to stop taking all that Vicodin, and six-packs on top of it," she said. "I told him it made him like a zombie. He's just out there sulking. A motel or something. I don't see how he could be driving very far, the way he gets."

Dad. The stable one in our family. Yeah, he used a lot of pills for his back pain, and he always had a beer going at home, but he didn't get comatose and he didn't get mean. He just got slowed down. And he could come out of it okay if Mom went on a tear.

Major problem he had was his work. No schedule. Long periods of nothing happening followed by some intense deal closing. He sold commercial pumps: irrigation, wells, circulating pumps for factory machinery. Most years he made a fair amount of money on commission.

He'd been the only salesman for Carbondale Pumps in northern California for years. He traveled some, drumming up business. He had his own contacts, and his laptop kept him current on inventory and e-mail orders, so I guess if he wanted to take a couple of weeks off, he could. No big deal. But when he was living at home, whenever he went on the road, he always packed his bags and took them with him. I didn't like the sound of Dad leaving empty-handed and not coming back.

I thanked Charlene and got off the phone to make a circuit of our house. Make sure the red candles weren't setting anything on fire. So far everything was okay, and I found Mom in the hall closet, sitting on the floor and singing hymns. Her voice wasn't great but I didn't think it would drive Lizards away.

"You better get in here," Mom said. "I don't know if the cross will hold them."

"Yeah, okay," I told her. "I'll be with you in a minute. I'm just making sure the windows are tight and the candles are safe. You go ahead." She started singing again and I closed the door.

I called Dad's work number. Maybe he'd found another woman and told the office people not to tell Charlene anything. I had met Dad's boss and I thought he'd tell me the truth. When he came on the line, Mr. Tracy said he hadn't seen or talked to Dad for the past week. He thought Dad was on a road trip through Siskiyou County because that area was next on his schedule, but he hadn't called in for any parts or sales confirmations, which was unusual. "Things must be pretty dead," he concluded.

I decided to take the car and check every motel in town. Probably Dad was holed up.

Mom first. I went to the bathroom to check the garbage can. Nobody ever empties it until it begins to spill over onto the floor. Down about the middle, I found Mom's current antipsychotic meds. I knew she was also supposed to be taking Klonopin to knock down anxiety, and I didn't think she'd toss that. I checked the medicine cabinet. Yep, the Klonopin was there, along with some old Ativan, and the sleepers: Dalmane and Ambien.

I took an Ativan and two Ambien to crush and put in mom's soda. She was tough to figure. The last time she went nuts, I tried to sedate her with Everclear in her fruit juice. Oops. Instead of falling asleep, she decided to drive to the sheriff's office and knocked down our mailbox and our neighbor's bay tree before I got her out from behind the wheel. I was hoping the Ativan would slow her down and the Ambien would put her out for a few hours.

Mom was very suspicious of medication, having had some pretty rough times in the hospitals. I couldn't just hand her the meds. Back in the kitchen, I mashed the pills between two spoons, keeping an eye on the closet door. I poured the powder into a glass of Mom's favorite, Coke Classic, and added extra lemon to cover the taste.

"Check the back porch," Mom told me when I opened the closet again.

I handed her the doctored soda.

"I think that's how they got in last time," she said, taking a long drink. "Do you still have that red T-shirt?"

"Yeah," I said. "I'll put it on in a sec."

She was looking over my shoulder, distracted by the bars of light the venetian blinds cast against the far wall.

"Hey," I said. "You're going to need liquids if you're going to be on watch today. Finish the Coke and I'll bring you a bottle of water."

When I came back, she handed me the empty glass, and I handed her a liter of water and the pillows and blankets I'd brought to make her more comfortable.

"You keep singing and I'll take care of the other stuff in the house."

"Unscrew the lightbulbs," she said. "I don't want them listening to us when we talk. And Ben?"

I stopped and waited for her to speak.

"Whatever you do, don't turn on the TV."

"You got it," I said.

Tough life. All your appliances are out to get you.

Twenty minutes later, when I looked in on her, Mom was dozing. I dug the car keys out of her purse and went to look for Dad. I didn't think he would spring for something expensive, but I checked the Hilton, Holiday Inn, and Red Lion parking lots first, then the other motels on Hillside Drive, then the cheap places on 273, and finally the downtown places on Main. No sign of his car.

Next the bars. Nothing at the Tropicana or Dave's Blue Light Club, the Coop, or any of the other dives I drove by. I know Dad doesn't like to drink in restaurants or pizza places. I was ready to give up, when I remembered the Pit, five miles north in Lake Vista. "A good pour," is how Dad had described it when we drove by one day. Right. His car was parked around the rear where the blacktop gave way to weeds. Hidden from the street.

He was in a back corner near the storeroom, with his laptop and a bottle of beer on the table in front of him. The booth was dark. I couldn't see his face. He was scribbling on some papers beside the computer. He didn't look up till I sat down.

"Ben," he said, but he didn't seem particularly surprised.

"Hi, Dad. How are you doing?"

"What brings you in here?" he asked, signaling the heavyset bleach-blond bartender and mouthing the word "Coke" at her.

"Mom is going off. It started again this morning with the red and the candles. I need your help."

"What do you expect me to do?" he asked, but he didn't seem to care about the answer. He was looking away, over to the bar, and holding up two fingers like he wanted a double for himself.

"Come on, Dad, I can't get her admitted to any hospital without you. You can at least take Mom into the unit and ask them to evaluate her."

"I'm done with your mom," he said, as if that was the last word on the matter.

"She's still your wife," I reminded him. "You have to help me. There's nothing else I can do by myself."

He pursed his lips. "Okay," he said. "I got to whiz and then we'll finish these drinks I just ordered and then we'll go home." He stood up and headed around the bar, toward the restrooms.

I was restless. Any minute Mom was going to wake up and the home situation would escalate to the next level. That could be anything: neighbors, police, firemen, even a local news team.

The waitress served his double whatever-it-was and my Coke, gave me a crumpled smile, and went back to the bar. I began to wonder where Dad was. It didn't usually take him this long to shower, shave, and dress at home.

I went to the men's room.

Empty.

I ran outside. His car was gone. Gone. Damn him. Lazy, good-for-nothing bastard! I wanted to punch him.

I headed home.

When I got there, Mom wouldn't let me in.

"You're infected," she yelled through the door.

Lizard pox?

I left and went to the police station.

Danger to Self

"**My** mom has stopped taking her medication, and she's a danger to herself and others," I told the policeman behind the counter at the station.

His face didn't have any expression. I guess you get that way working behind the counter in a police station. He waited for me to go on.

"She has locked the house and won't let me in, and my dad won't come help get her admitted."

Still the old stoneface.

"She's been admitted before, here and in Sacramento." I was trying to think of the right words to get

him to do something. "Uh, I'm her son, and I'm request-
ing a safety-and-welfare check on Mrs. Noreen Mander,
3212 Sandie Lane."

"Name?" No change in expression, but at least Stoneface was finally speaking.

"Noreen—"

"Your name?"

"Ben Mander."

"Residence?"

"Same place," I said. "I'm a student at Sierra High."

"Take a seat, please," he said, and nodded toward
some wooden chairs against the side wall. "An officer will
be with you shortly." The man's attention shifted to the
next person in line behind me.

The patrolman was huge. He looked like a blue wool
mountain. "Mander?" he said.

"Yes." I stood up.

The man's face was round, bisected by a sparse black
mustache. He yawned.

"Your mother has destabilized?" he said, but it didn't
really sound like a question. "This is, what, the third
time in the past couple of months?"

"Second or third," I said.

"Has she been drinking or using street drugs?" he
asked.

"I don't think so," I said. "Really, I guess, uh, I don't
know. I think just benzodiazepines, uh, you know, an-
tianxiety stuff like Klonopin."

"Any guns in the house?"

"No. She's not exactly dangerous," I said. "She hits and bites when she's afraid and cornered, but she doesn't actually try to hurt people."

"She's locked herself in your home?"

"Yes."

"You have a car?"

I nodded.

"I'm going to meet the mental health liaison at your house in ten minutes. We'll probably take your mother to the hospital for an emergency evaluation. Meet us at the hospital in thirty minutes. Don't go back home. You'll just be in the way." He rubbed the bridge of his nose with a thick finger, like he was thinking how complicated this might get. "I know this is rough on you," he said. "Don't worry. We won't hurt her." He looked me in the eyes. "I mean it."

He was out the door before I could think of anything to say.

Something's Happened

Marco! Marco was sitting in the admitting area of the hospital when I walked in. I recognized him right away.

"Something's happened to me," he said without looking up.

I looked at him closer. He looked kind of shaggy, but I couldn't see any injury.

"What do you mean?" I asked him, wondering if he would suggest I sit down beside him. I gave the room a quick scan to make sure Mom hadn't arrived yet.

He looked up again, looked around the lobby.

I didn't see the self-confidence that had been so obvious when we first met. Now he seemed tense.

"It has to do with this illness thing," he said. "I don't want to talk about it here."

"I think my mom's going to be admitted again," I told him. "When that gets done, I could probably meet you somewhere."

I thought about suggesting he come to my house, but I didn't. I figured he'd understand. This was a thing about having a strange mom. You couldn't exactly invite someone to your home whenever you wanted to, because you were never sure what you would find when you opened the front door. Mom covered in lipstick singing hymns in the closet? Not so good.

"Ah," he said, "you don't want to hear about all this stuff. This is nuts. It can't help anybody."

"Try me," I said.

We had just agreed to meet at his house later that night, when Mom came in between Man-mountain and the gray-haired County Mental Health woman. Mom's lipstick was now smeared all over her face, and her hair was mussed like she had been in a struggle. The mountain was also a little worse for wear. He had puffy red scratches on the plains of his cheeks and a white tape bandage on his right hand. Mom was trying to pull away but they had her in a firm grip. When Mom saw me, she started crying.

I stood to the side while the caseworker requested an evaluation. The big cop and an RN who was large enough to have been his sister took Mom down the hall. The social worker stayed in the waiting room. I knew her. She had visited our home before, assigned by the county to oversee our "case." I don't think she saw me. She was busy jotting something down in a black notebook. I looked around to see what Marco thought of all this, but he had slipped away.

I wondered how long Mom would be staying. I thought she would probably get at least a forty-eight-hour hold for being what they called a "danger to others," maybe longer if they were going to start a new medication.

The patrolman returned. "Are you eighteen?"

I shook my head.

"Then the liaison, Betty Lou, will sign if your mother has to be admitted, but I don't think she will be. I'm guessing they'll look at her and give her some medication and let her go."

"Let Mom go? That won't work. She'll be back here in less than twenty-four hours." I went straight to the admitting station, to the male clerk with the thick black glasses.

"You can't let Mom go," I interrupted his conversation with the liaison lady. "There's no one home but me to take care of her, and I have to go to school."

It took an hour. In the end, the hospital would not admit Mom because our insurance wouldn't cover her stay. It would, instead, hold her for twelve hours or so, to monitor her response to the dose of medication they were giving her. Betty Lou would make a daily check on Mom and me for the following week to make sure our home was safe and secure. This, too, had happened a few times before. Mom would probably take her medication as prescribed until Betty Lou stopped coming around, and then, same old, same old.

Man-mountain's radio squawked and he informed Betty Lou he had to leave.

He turned to me.

"Things get bad later this week or next week, give me a call and I'll see what I can do," he said, taking a card out of his shirt pocket. "Ask for Dullborne."

I watched him walk out, turning to the side to get through a door that was built to accommodate gurneys. Dullborne. I bet nobody teased him about his name.

I drove Betty Lou back to our house to pick up her car. Betty Lou set up tomorrow's visit. She gave me her card, too. Watching her drive away, I thought, Okay, I've got two new cards, but nothing's really been fixed. Hey, not a bad idea. Got a problem? Get a card! I could have some business cards printed, and whenever Mom lost it, I could hand her one. Is this whole world crazy? Hey! I deserve another card!

I hurried to clean up the red crepe paper and ribbons in case they let Mom go early. Maybe if she didn't see the red stuff, she wouldn't think about the Lizards for a while.

I Couldn't See
My Hand

Marco's neighborhood was an unfinished subdivision on the northeast end of town by the freeway. Four or five blocks of look-alike three-bedroom homes. In the quarter-moon light, most of the rest of it appeared to be scrub trees in fields of dead grass. Breezes off the nearby Cascades pushed branches and moved the grass in slow waves.

His house looked barely lived in. Carpet but no furniture in the living room. No TV. No couch. I could see appliances like a stove and fridge, but no table in the kitchen, no dishes in the sink. Three wooden chairs in what I imagined was the dining room.

I followed him into his room. The walls were covered with detailed posters of stars and galaxies. His bed was a mattress on the floor with two pillows and a sleeping bag on top of it. He saw me looking.

"Don't like doing laundry," he explained. He leaned against a wall and looked out the window into his backyard.

The floor was strewn with piles of news magazines and notebooks. I didn't see a computer. I don't know anyone who doesn't have a computer. There were no clothes on the floor, no books, no clock radio or CD player, no candy wrappers, no soda cans.

Marco brought in one of the dining-room chairs and put it facing his bed. He plopped down again, waited for me to sit, and started.

"I found something." He stopped. Began again. "My mom's crazy, right? For a long time I've been wondering how to help her. I walk a lot. Zone out. Think. Try to figure things out. Worry. Stuff like that. Whatever. I always look at birds and trees and pets and kids playing and stuff. We haven't been here that long, but anyway, around here is a pretty large oak tree." He nodded toward the window, to the field in back of his house. "I don't know why I kind of fixed on it. Live oaks are pretty interesting. Some keep their leaves year-round. You people give out bronze or gold oak leaves for military decorations, like for repeated acts of bravery."

You people?

"Branches so big and thick they almost block out the sun," he continued. "Makes a neat hangout. Like a natural tent. We never had them where I grew up. So, a couple of weeks ago, just messing around, I went inside by the trunk. I was actually thinking Indians from this area could have used a tree like that for shelter. You know. I was scanning the ground, wondering if I might even find an arrowhead. Anyway, near the back of the trunk, something weird was happening. There was this pattern like you see sometimes above the blacktop on a real hot day. A heat mirage, all wavy, distorting the light? And I was close enough to put my hand through it and . . . and, uh, when I did, I couldn't see it at the end of my wrist."

I had shut my eyes, trying to picture what he was describing. When he stopped speaking, I opened them.

He had turned his head at an angle and narrowed his eyes. Assessing. "Do you believe me?" He wanted to know.

I was unprepared. I had just been listening. Curious. Just trying to visualize what he was saying and trying to remember whether Indians ever used live oaks for shelter and what the trunks looked like, and trying to remember the last time I had been inside a canopy of branches like that. I realized my mouth was open, and I shut it.

"Well?" he asked, not letting me off the hook.

"I don't know," I said, which was true. "I'm just listening. Go on."

He looked in my eyes for what seemed like a pretty long time, like he was trying to decide about me. Probably wondering whether I would use whatever he was going to say against him. I wasn't like that. But how could he know?

"Hey," I said. "You met me at a psych hospital. You know the kind of stuff I go through with my mother." It wasn't clear to me exactly what I meant by that, except maybe that he and I were struggling with the same kind of situation. I wanted his trust.

He put his hands together, almost like a meditation thing, and closed his eyes and started speaking in the third person.

That threw me for a minute until I remembered ESPN interviews where famous athletes talked about themselves and their lives using the third person—as if they had become their own story instead of their own self.

"Whoa, wait a minute," I interrupted him. "I got spaced for a second. Start again, please."

"Okay," he said. He didn't seem impatient. "You remember that I stuck my hand in the wavy area and couldn't see it anymore?"

"Yeah, I followed you to there."

"It turned out to be a wormhole," he said. "Or a time portal. Or like string theory, another dimension, a parallel universe."

4000

By the year 4000, the climate had gotten much warmer, and in the city where Marco exited, people were mostly slender and everybody had coffee-colored skin decorated with bright tattoos or paintings. Outdoors, they wore a lot of variations on what people today call swimsuits, and they all had decorative earpieces with thin wire jewelry arranged around their cheeks and ending near their mouths. Telephones?

The buildings were smooth and rounded, spheres and oblongs of different sizes, but they didn't have signs. Maybe the shapes were supposed to tell you what they were. Or those symbols outside the doors could have really been signs, like logos or something. Maybe each building had everything anyone needed: shops and apartments and restaurants and movies and doctors.

The portal let Marco out beside a massive cedar tree in the middle of a field. A park? And people were gliding around on what looked like skateboards with a cane sticking up in front to hold on to. But there were no wheels and no motor.

While Marco was looking around, a small metal disk like a hockey puck whacked into him and bit him. Well, not bit him exactly, but attached itself to his shirtsleeve and began flashing a message on a small screen. Marco couldn't pull the disk off, and he couldn't read the message. It was a series of lines that looked liked unfinished letters grouped into words. ∪/--∧--૨--?∪/---∧-- →?. . .∪/--∧--૨--?∪/---∧-- →? There was a blinking blue button at the end of the screen, and Marco pushed it but nothing seemed to happen.

When he looked up, several silver tube things, each about a foot in diameter and a yard long, were gliding toward him a couple of feet off the ground. The lead one had a flexible hose extending from the front of it. Trouble! He tore off his shirt and jammed back into the portal.

Just as he had a few minutes ago, he was rocketing through a tunnel, like one of those huge metal culverts, with brilliant red lines zinging along the walls. Fireworks shot into his vision, his skin was electrified, and then he was just standing back in the present, under the oak tree, like nothing had happened.

Whoa! Talk about a roller coaster! Where had he been? Scary, but what a rush! One of a kind, right? He bet no one had done anything like this before. He might be the next Magellan! He pictured his name in lights in Times Square. Marco Lasalle discovers . . . what? A new country? A new planet?

Marco was better prepared next time. He put on a heavy jacket so that when the metal disk struck, he could take off the jacket and wrap the thing inside it. He figured if he didn't press the blue button, and if he kept moving, he could find somebody to talk to. Also, he decided to go at night, when it might be easier to explore undetected.

The field was dark and there were just as many people gliding around as when he visited before. The gliders carried their own glow and illuminated the area around them wherever they went. In a few seconds the puck glommed onto him, and he caught it in his jacket, as he had planned. He began chasing nearby gliders, but whenever he got close, they speeded up and stayed just out of his reach. He waved at people and they waved back. They didn't stop.

When he was tired, he rested under the tree, but when he looked up, he could see the whole night sky. It was just a projection of a tree, transparent from the inside. He caught his breath and walked to a building.

He followed a sidewalk-type path to the front wall, and when he got a couple of feet away, a section of wall slid back. He went inside. The floor was a glossy tile that didn't make any noise when you walked on it. Immediately in front of him were a series of terminals that looked like computers on stalks.

Marco figured that this was where you got your directions. He walked to the nearest one and put his fingers on the keyboard. The keys were in the same script that had been flashing on the metal disk. He moved the cursor to the open address box at the top of the screen, closed his eyes, and tried typing using the key positions he knew. He typed "Google.com" and hit what he thought was the "Enter" key.

While Marco was watching the screen, he felt a poke on his arm. A tube with a hose had attached to him. He gave a tug to break loose, but it did no good. The tube made a noise like a short song in a foreign language.

"I don't understand," Marco told it.

A tiny door opened in the top of the tube and a plain earphone and wire mike pushed out. Marco put them on.

"Who are you?" he heard when the earphone was in place.

"Marco Lasalle."

"What are you doing here?"

"I'm, uh, I'm a visitor. I'm looking . . . for a cure. For mental illness," Marco said, trying to make it sound like his business here was important. "Not for me," he added, but he didn't think anyone heard him. The machine was already leading Marco out the door and over to a waiting skateboard—floatboard? Marco stepped onto it and began gliding through the city at high speed.

Once away from the park, there were lots of people gliding but no cars in the streets. Everything was spotlessly clean. No paper, no trash, no plastic bags caught on trees or bushes. No trees or bushes! The machine stopped abruptly near the entrance of a huge building that looked like four blimps joined together at their noses. A steady stream of people was going in and coming out. The gliders, or floatboards, were parked in a line along the edge of the walk. The tube led Marco inside to a front desk. Service counter? Nursing station?

The person ahead finished, and the tube propelled Marco forward. A large-chested middle-aged woman in a light blue apron uniform looked him over carefully.

"How can I help you?"

Marco heard her clearly, though those words didn't seem to match the words her lips formed. Then he heard what sounded like another foreign song, this, he thought, from the tube.

The woman's eyebrows lifted. "Wait here," she said. She leaned her head down to her shoulder and sang something to a button that rested there. The tube pulled Marco to the side so the person next in line could step up.

In less than a minute, a light blue metallic tube came and attached to Marco. The silver tube let go and left. Light Blue led Marco at a leisurely pace down a long corridor, past a series of doors. Beside most of the doors were chairs, and sometimes people sat in them as if waiting for an appointment.

After a right turn into a perpendicular hall, the tube stopped in front of the nearest door and emitted a tone. The door opened and Marco was escorted inside. The tube released him and left. A coffee-colored man in a blue smock with black piping was waiting. He had five stripes where a chest pocket would have been, with a row of small medallions beneath. He was in his thirties or forties. Cleft-chinned, handsome, dapper, no smile. He combed his hair in a complicated arrangement of swirls. Marco wondered if the man was really conceited.

"Are you loose?" the man asked.

"I'm not sure," Marco said.

"Then you are loose," the man said. The man pressed a button on the console he was standing behind. The silver tube returned.

"Take him back to the University," the man told it.

"I didn't come from there," Marco said.

"None of us did," the man said, barely concealing a smile.

"What is this place? Where are we? Is this a hospital?" Marco asked him.

"Are you saying you're one of our patients?" the man asked.

"No," Marco said. "I'm just visiting, and I want . . . uh, I need to find your cure for mental illness."

"So you are one of ours," the man said. He sang something to the tube and it turned and projected a zoom-in of Marco in the park, Marco chasing gliders, Marco standing in front of the terminal in the other building.

The man sang again, and the tube clamped onto Marco's arm. "You'll go to Dr. Gila on the second floor," he said.

"You don't understand." Marco tugged at the tube. "It's not for me! It's for my mom. I arrived here through a tunnel, a space tunnel that let me out in that park you just saw. I just came out near that tree. Right before I started chasing the gliders."

"I understand," the man said. "That's what they all say."

I kept listening, deep in the story, maybe like a trance, eyes closed, but in another part of my mind, questions accumulated. *A cure for mental illness? The year 4000?* Has he gone nuts on me?

Dr. Gila was a tall, blunt-featured, muscular woman in a pale blue jacket and skirt and matching sandals. Her whole outfit was edged in black, and she had some stripes and medallions, too. She was standing in front of her console, her hands folded in front of her. She waited for Marco to speak.

"I don't need this," Marco told her. "I'm trying to help my mom is all. I'm okay."

She looked compassionate, patient. It was probably her eyes.

"I came here because I found a wormhole, a time-portal deal, and I thought you people seemed really advanced. You might know lots of things . . . uh, how to cure diseases or how to cure mental illness . . . and my mom and other people need help."

"Is this the role they gave you at the University?" she asked. "Are you in premed or psychometry?"

"I don't know about any University," Marco said. "I don't even know what you call this place. I'm from Riverton. California."

"Of course," she said. "So you won't mind if I connect to the University for some information?"

Marco didn't know what to say.

The woman stood very straight, very still. Her hands raised and opened in front of her, framing her face, fingers pointing toward the ceiling. The flesh around the bridge of her nose began a slow swelling, blunting her features, and her complexion, even her hands, took on a scaly bronze-green coloration, something like the skin of a reptile.

Marco jumped back, but the woman didn't seem to notice. She had closed her eyes and started a thin, high-pitched, atonal whistle. She stopped and waited. Whistled again for a minute or so. Waited, listening, and then she opened her eyes and lowered her hands. The swelling dissipated and her skin returned to its normal texture and light coffee color.

I couldn't seem to interrupt his monologue. I was kind of trapped, but curious.

"The University confirms," she said. "You're not registered. And, Dr. Monitor on the first floor tells me you have no chart with us. Do you have a supervising caregiver in this city or are you a transfer?"

"How can I get you to believe me?" Marco asked her, aware that his voice sounded whiny.

"I'll believe you the minute you start telling me the truth or making sense," she said.

"Give me a lie-detector test," Marco said.

"All right," she said.

A small black cube entered the room from the side and attached to the back of Marco's head. It began making sounds like an electronic soprano recorder, and a video image appeared on the wall behind the console. It began with a pan of the oak tree. Next, a pan of a house with red paper stuffed everywhere, red cloth hanging from lamps, and a red Celtic cross in the front hall.

The doctor sang a loud, sharp note, and the picture dissolved. "God, I hate that color!" she said, rubbing her eyes like they burned.

*   *   *

45

"Stop!" I didn't mean to yell, but I was breathing hard. My eyes were wide open. "Stop," I said again in a softer voice. "What are you doing?" I was trying to keep myself from either punching him or running out of his house. "What are you saying? Where did you get that story?"

Marco continued to sit in his meditative position. "I'm just telling you what happened to me. You said you wanted to hear it. Do you want me to stop?"

He was so calm. This afternoon he'd been nervous, but now he was like a monk.

"How did you know about the red stuff, the cross?" I asked him, still trying to get my breathing back to normal.

"I'm just telling you what went on. Do you want me to shut it off? Not tell you any more?"

I did. I really did. Not another word!

"No," I said, "keep talking."

"All right," Dr. Gila said, and the video resumed.

The scene moved to the closet, to a woman with red forehead and chin, swaying, grimacing, hands pressed over her ears, singing.

The video was interrupted by a silver tube entering the room and handing the doctor Marco's leather jacket, which was making a series of loud clicks. The doctor unfolded it and the metal puck floated up to her eye level, stopped clicking, made some tones, and then glided out with the tube.

The doctor sang a short phrase and the black box beeped.

When the box left, the doctor went around to the back of her console and sat down. She took a deep breath and sat looking down in the direction of some sliding switches beside her keyboard. Thinking.

"This is serious," she said, not looking up. "How long have you had this condition?"

Marco ran.

But not far enough.

4000 Treatment

Marco was put in a room where one whole wall was a window looking out on some kind of wildlife preserve. The room itself was small and comfortable, with a bed and overstuffed chair. There was a toilet and a shower behind a translucent curtain, and a sink and refrigerator thing that dispensed ice and cold water. Fruit and rolls sat in a basket on the table. Somehow—was it magnetism?—none of the furniture would move, not even the basket. The room had its own daylight, and it smelled like it was right next to a waterfall.

Beside the basket on the table was a floating computer screen, but you could see through it like the tree Marco had stood under in the field. On the table under the screen was a button outlined by amber light. Marco pressed it and the screen lit, but nothing else happened. He let it go and the screen resumed its previous state.

Marco sat on the edge of the bed and looked out the window. Brightly colored birds flew tree to tree. Very large gray squirrels darted across the grounds, up trunks, and into branches. Auburn deer with white streaks on their sides grazed or slept on the rough blue-green grass. Flower gardens on the far perimeter. The sky was a vivid blue. Marco felt his ear. The translator thing was still in place.

Back at the screen, he pressed the amber button and spoke. "Where am I?"

The screen had a soothing voice. " Sector Four One Zero Five Interborough Health Conglomerate."

"What does that mean?" Marco asked.

After a pause, the screen said, "Ask a more specific question, please."

"What is the purpose of this place?"

"Regional center for human healing," the screen said.

"I'm not sick," Marco said.

Silence.

"I need help," Marco said.

Silence.

"What year is this?"

"4000."

"How do you cure mental illness?" Marco asked.

"How would you like to be cured?" the screen asked.

"I don't . . . What are my choices?"

"Accept it and do nothing, take compounds to restore optimal brain function, consent to electro-stim surgery." The screen was pausing briefly between each option. "Live communally with others possessing similar proclivities, undergo radical organ exchange, authorize yearly psychotropic injections, attend University support interventions for enculturative skill-building—"

"What would be the purpose?"

"Developing tools to cope with perceptual differences." The screen paused again. "Sign up for glandular implants and genetic reprogramming, wear portable neurotransmitter enhancement devices, and, of course, see an integration counselor if you wish."

Marco considered these options.

"Are you ready to begin?" the screen asked.

"I actually live a ways from here," Marco said. "What could you give me that I could take with me?"

"How far away?" the screen asked.

"Two thousand years."

"I'm afraid you will need to stay here a while longer," the screen said.

The next day the window showed an ocean tide pool with the lowest two feet featuring the underwater view. Anemones waved, hermit crabs scurried, starfish clung to their rocks. From time to time a cod or some rockfish scooted by.

"I may have been asking the wrong question," Marco said, "because you keep thinking that I'm the person who needs help. I'm not. I'm looking for help for other people. Please tell me how a person who lived in 2007 could fix mental illness."

The screen stayed quiet for a few seconds. "Do you mean, what was the cure for mental illness in the year 2007?" it asked.

"Sure," Marco said.

"Where?"

"In California, the United States, uh, Earth."

"I am sorry," the screen responded. "I am unable to access primitive records. But I have a speculation," it said. "Would you like to hear it?"

"None?" Marco said.

The screen remained silent.

The next day the window showed a high mountain lake, fir-covered banks, fish jumping, nesting eagles, no underwater view.

"What is the purpose of the window?" Marco asked the screen.

"Treatment," the screen responded. "Quieting, grounding. An aesthetic focus to displace anxiety and confusion, should you choose."

"How do I get out of here?" Marco asked.

"I think you know," the screen said.

"What if your system has made a mistake?" Marco asked.

"Prove it," the screen said.

After a while, I realized that Marco had finished talking. I don't know what time it was. Late. I opened my eyes. Marco's were closed. I was spooked. I had so many questions, but I had to get out of there. I had to think. I left without saying a word.

Out in my car, I sat with my hands on the wheel but I didn't start the engine. There was a glow that illuminated the fields. Reflected city lights, maybe, I couldn't find the moon. A wormhole, I thought. Yeah, and I'm Bill Gates. I don't think so. Is a thing like a time portal or another dimension even possible? I would ask Hubie. And how did Marco know about the Lizards and the red, about Mom's delusion? I turned the radio on and turned it right off again. Shook the steering wheel. Tried to relax my jaw. It didn't help.

I don't know whether you push things out of your mind because you just don't know how to deal with them, or whether that's a good habit or a bad habit. But it's what I did right then with the story Marco had told me.

When I got home I sat in a chair in the living room in the dark, looking out the window at the empty street and the shadows that shifted and leaned like ghosts marching.

Surveillance

I woke up thinking about school and feeling kind of sorry for myself. Some junior year, worried every day that Mom would go off. I rarely thought about school, even when I was there, and just did enough homework to get by. My grades had all dropped to Cs since Dad left. I wanted to give up. Just quit. Get baked and go for a low-altitude record. Maybe that's what Dad did. Maybe he was the smart one.

A memory pooled in my mind. I don't know where it came from. I saw Mom screaming, twisting in Dad's arms. He had her pinned standing up, his hands clasped tight so she couldn't get a hand free and hit him. Her eyes were wild, and she was spitting and cursing and yelling that we were all going to be killed.

I was eight or nine and I remember my head was buzzing. I couldn't get hold of what I was seeing. *"What's the matter with Mom?"* I kept yelling that, kept asking again and again, and Dad was yelling back, *"Nothing! Go to your room. Go on! Go back to sleep!"* A broken record, until he got hold of the keys and pulled Mom kicking and screaming out the front door. I heard the car start but I didn't move. Just stood there. Stood there until my eyes got tired, and then went back to my bedroom.

We didn't talk about it. Ever. Haven't still. I remembered the feeling, like the earth had come apart. Feeling that my family was disintegrating right in front of me. I didn't think anything would ever be the same again. But I remember Dad fixed us breakfast the next day and said Mom was visiting people and wouldn't be home for a few days. And that was that. I did the push-it-out-of-your-mind trick, and I don't think I thought of it again until this morning. And now I had a cramp that got me running to the bathroom.

Before I left for school Wednesday, I called the police and asked for Patrolman Dullborne. He wasn't in yet, so I left him a message asking if he would meet me at school that afternoon. The phone rang as soon as I had set it back in its cradle. Hubie.

"Heard you had a little more trouble yesterday," he said.

"Yeah," I said, "Mom's back on the Lizard thing." I reached up to rub at my hair, wishing I had taken the time to shower this morning. "She's not too bad, I guess. They didn't admit her, just held her awhile to restart her medications, so she'll probably be coming home sometime early afternoon."

"My mom said to tell you to let us know if there's anything we can do to help."

I could hear Mrs. Ludlow's voice in the background. "Thanks, Hube. And tell her thanks, too." How did the Ludlows always seem to know when my mom was off the beam? I bet the local nursing grapevine. "I'll be all right," I told him. "Betty Lou whats-her-name from the County is helping us. I'll see how Mom's doing when I get home from school."

After I hung up, I remembered something that Dullborne had asked me. I wondered about the drugs. Has Mom been using something else to make herself feel better? She used to do pot every day until her doctor told Dad that it was interfering with her psych meds, changed the brain chemistry balance that enabled her to think right. Dad and I had searched the house and gotten rid of her stash, and since then, I had been pretty sensitive to any marijuana smell around the place. I didn't think she'd been back to pot again. But something else? I wondered if she had any visitors lately when I'd been at school. Hmmm.

I could ask Mr. Bellarmine next door. I knew he had retired sometime last year. His wife had cancer and died a couple of years before that, and now he lived alone and kept a pretty good eye on the neighborhood. Mom had called him a snoop. Of course, Mom was paranoid. I thought it was kind of early to go across the driveway and knock on his door, but I figured I'd do it anyway. If I had Mr. Bellarmine pegged right, he'd been up and organized since dawn.

"Visitor?" Mr. Bellarmine asked, his brow creasing. "Who? That long-haired bozo in the black car? I thought he was just delivering liquor. She's not supposed to have liquor, is she? Never buttons his shirt? Those motorcycle boots? I never liked that look." He was standing in his doorway, holding the screen open. "Come in if you'd like," he said.

He looked like he was dressed for work, in a sport-coat, gray hair carefully combed, shoes shined. He caught me sizing him up.

"It doesn't do for a person to let himself go, just because he's retired," he said, explaining, not apologizing. "Want breakfast?" he asked.

I shook my head.

This visitor was not good news.

Dullborne got me out of Chemistry, which was great, because I was lost somewhere in the nomenclature of inorganic compounds. We walked away from the classroom and over by the stairs, where we had some privacy.

"Thanks," I said. "It's about my dad. I found him in a bar between here and Lake City, but I've already talked to him once, and I don't think he'll come home and deal with Mom unless you make him."

Dullborne took off his dark blue patrol hat, ran his hand over his hair, and put the hat back on. "I can't do that," he said. "It's not legal. It's not even my jurisdiction. That's County. Sheriff's department. But it doesn't make much difference, because they won't do it either. A law officer can't make your father come home and take care of business." He shifted his weight. "A sheriff could arrest him if there was a warrant out for a crime your dad committed, but I don't think that would help you any, unless maybe it wound up getting your mom some back child-support money. The law can't really force anyone to behave like a good husband or father."

I tried to mask my disappointment. "But, uh, but I thought you said to call you if I needed help."

"With your mother," he said. "I can help you if your mother gets out of control and becomes a danger to herself or others, but I can't help you with your father unless he breaks the law. I'm sorry. Has Betty Lou followed through?"

"I don't know. Maybe. She's supposed to come by later today and see that Mom's settled in okay. She might still be there when I get home from school."

"Yeah, well, I got to go. Sorry I couldn't be much help."

"No, yeah, I mean, I understand. Thanks for coming by. One more thing?"

He waited.

"If a guy was giving Mom street drugs, would you arrest him or scare him off? I mean, you asked me before if she was using drugs. Maybe she is. Would you help with that?"

He was rubbing the bridge of his nose again.

"We'll see," he said. "Call me if you find out something for sure."

I watched him walk down the stairs to the ground floor. Now what was I supposed to do?

Vice Principal Onabi answered that question. "Get back to class!"

Rude, Blued, and Tattooed

When I got home after school, a guy was sitting on our couch. While I was standing in the front hall, looking at him, Mom came in from the kitchen and handed him a can of beer. She saw me when she sat beside him. Her eyes were red and didn't seem focused. She was still wearing yesterday's clothes. She looked away quickly and brushed her hands against her jeans, a thing she often did when she was nervous.

"Ben," she said. Her voice was rough, probably left over from screaming at Dullborne. "Ben," she repeated, "I'm sorry."

I didn't answer. She always felt embarrassed when the police had to take her in.

I had so many feelings. I was mad at her for stopping her meds and getting crazy again. Sorry for her. I knew she felt humiliated.

I didn't know what to say. This was the third time we'd played this scene this year. Nothing I could say would do any good. She'd promised lots of times that she would take care of herself and do what the doctors told her to. I felt like yelling, and I felt like crying. I wouldn't do either in front of this guy.

I felt like slapping her. As if hurting her physically would knock some sense into her. Right. And an image passed through my mind like a commercial. I was in my room packing. Taking the few things that mattered to me anymore: the photo of Mom and Dad, the framed academic award I got for being the top of my seventh-grade class, my first-place sophomore wrestling trophy, and my fly rod. And then I was walking out the front door, going to live with Hubie. Sweet!

The guy caught my attention, shifting his position on the couch. He hadn't looked at me. He kept staring at the wall across from him like it had a newspaper taped to it, or maybe he could see out the window and there was something fascinating happening on the lawn.

I didn't say anything and neither did he. Mr. Bellarmine had been right. He was wearing heavy boots and his shirt was open. He also had tattoos all over his arms, and he was outhouse ugly.

I walked to the coffee table.

"What are you doing here?" I said, a hard edge in my voice.

He looked at me then. Like I was a bug that had lit in his food. He stood up. He was an inch or two taller than me, but probably didn't weigh as much. Wasted, thin, with a little pot gut. He had scars around his eyes. Broken glass? Knife? And the teeth I could see were stained yellow and brown, at least one missing from both top and bottom. Scraggly mustache.

"Leaving," he said, and carried his beer out the door without another word or a backward glance at Mom.

"What's he doing here?" I asked Mom.

"Nothing," she said. She sounded real tired. Had to make an effort to speak. "Nothing. Came to see me." She didn't meet my eyes. "I'm tired." She made a gesture with her head toward the back of the house. "I'm going to bed."

"Are you doing drugs, Mom?" I could feel the shock wave as I said it. I don't know if she could.

She looked at me then. Shook her head. "I'm feeling pretty groggy."

"Do you remember yesterday?" I asked her.

"You don't think people are trying to kill me, but they are," she said, her eyes growing brighter. "They're broadcasting. You pretend you don't hear it, but you know who they are. Doctors think they can knock me out so I'll forget about it. Well, as soon as you forget, they've got you. If it wasn't for me, you and your dad would already be switched."

Mom's face sharpened and she looked more intense

when she talked like this. The doctors said it wouldn't work to argue with her about these ideas. Strange ideas are a symptom of the illness, they said. The only treatment is regular doses of antipsychotic medication and a stable environment with as few stressors as possible. Right. And then Dad leaves her for another woman.

"Is that guy giving you drugs?" I asked her.

Her eyes flared. "Vinnie's my friend," she said, getting up. "My friend." She walked past me to her bedroom and closed the door.

That night . . . Why did I wait until dark? Why did I even go? I don't know. That night, I went back to Marco's house, got the dining room chair myself this time, and asked for more of the story.

4000

Marco knew he needed to get back to the portal. He thought if he could escape the hospital, if that's what it was, he could just keep going till he reached the park. He needed out of this room.

"I have to see Dr. Gila!" he yelled, and pounded on the door.

A little bit of white steam came out of a vent in the ceiling, and the next thing Marco knew, he was on the floor, feeling dizzy. Marco didn't see the door open but he felt the tube pulling on his arm. He heard some tonal clicking, but he couldn't understand it. He realized his earpiece had become dislodged when he fell. He found it and put it back in.

". . . me now. Come with me now," the machine was saying as it led him along the corridors back to Dr. Gila's office.

"I'm feeling better," he told her after the tube had exited.

"All right," she said. "Who are you?"

"I'm . . . My name is Newt. I'm a nephew of Dr. Monitor. That's why you don't have me in your records. He sent me over here to teach me a lesson." Marco watched Dr. Gila to see if she bought his story.

"That kind of teaching doesn't sound like the Dr. Monitor I know," the woman said, looking for something on her desk.

"Wait a minute!" he said, thinking this might be his last chance. "Okay, my name's not Newt. But here's the problem. When I told you the truth the last time, you didn't believe me. Give me a minute, and I'll explain the whole thing."

Dr. Gila leaned over and pressed a button on her desk.

"No!" Marco screamed. "I can explain!"

"Hold my calls," Dr. Gila said to a small pad below the button. Then she sat and looked at him. Waiting.

"Okay. First, I don't understand how it works, but I really did come through a wormhole or time connector of some sort. It's located over in a park or a field about a mile or two from here. Second. I'm . . . on a mission." Marco was starting to believe it himself. "I really do need to know what the cure for mental illness is. So I can help my Mom."

Where was his Mom? Where was his family? Was his Mom in the hospital all this time?

* * *

64

"I live in a state called California, in the year 2007," Marco explained. "I'm not crazy. I just wanted help and thought I might find it here in the future."

Dr. Gila smoothed wrinkles out of her sleeve. "California. I've not heard of that. An ancient state? This planet?"

Marco nodded. And then he realized he wasn't sure. This planet? He couldn't say exactly where he was or what had happened to him.

"We don't have anything like mental illness in 4000," she said. "Genetic engineering, glandular implants, and brain chemistry balancing devices have virtually eliminated it. When the rare case surfaces, the person is offered a variety of treatment options. Which one would you like?"

Marco was disappointed by the question. "I don't need one. There is nothing wrong with me!"

"Why did you tell me your name was Newt a minute ago?"

"Well, uh, because your name is Gila and the other doctor's name is Monitor and those are both lizards. And, I saw your face get different and your skin change when you whistled for information earlier and so I thought . . . uh, if I pretended I was a lizard, too, you might think I was okay."

"You think that I'm a lizard?" Dr. Gila leaned back in her chair.

"I, uh, yes," Marco said, feeling very off balance. Feeling less certain every second. "I think so. Aren't you?"

"Do you think a person can be a human being and a lizard at the same time?" The doctor made a steeple with her fingers.

"Um, no," Marco said, "I don't think so."

"So," Dr. Gila said, "let me ask you again. What kind of treatment would you like?"

Marco felt like his brain was being tied in knots and re-arranged into cornrows. The more he tried to tell the truth and make sense of his situation, the more confused he got. Now he wasn't sure of anything that had happened to him in this place. Did his window change each day? Or did he move to different locations? Was he in a building or on a ship of some kind? And was he talking to a person or a lizard?

"I need to talk to Dr. Monitor," Marco said. "I want to go to his office with you and I'll show you the entry or exit or whatever it is."

"Well, I want to talk with Dr. Monitor, too," Dr. Gila said. "But he's missing. No one has seen him since the day you were admitted."

"He's gone through the portal!" Marco practically yelled at Dr. Gila. "I told him about it. About how I got here. That's why you can't find him."

Dr. Gila was up and out of the room before Marco had even finished speaking.

She came back with a shot-putter of a woman wearing a yellow uniform that was covered with what Marco first thought were medals, but which turned out to be tools of all kinds.

"Show us what you call the portal," Dr. Gila said. It sounded like an order.

Yes! Marco tried not to let them see how eager he was. Practically free!

The woman in yellow took two different-sized buttons off her tunic and placed them on Marco's cheek. "Stabilizer and locator," his headset translated.

Marco didn't like the sound of that but had no time to protest as they briskly led him out to the street. A toboggan-type board slid up to them and both women stepped up on it. Marco joined them and it glided away immediately.

"The locator traces your spatial memory," Dr. Gila explained as they sped along in what Marco thought was the direction of the park.

And the stabilizer? Marco wondered.

Tonight I wasn't as uncomfortable as I'd been the night before. With my eyes closed, it was a little like being told a weird bedtime story. I could picture the whole thing as he spoke, like I was watching a movie. But in the back of my mind, I was computing. This can't be true, so what's going on here?

"The entry point is under the biggest branch a few feet from the trunk," Marco told the two women.

The big woman in yellow took a lie detector box off her belt and held it above her head. In less than a minute, a silver tube appeared. They sang to each other, but Marco didn't get a translation. Yellow took a small cylinder out of her pants pocket, and it unrolled to form a screen. The silver tube began projecting onto it.

The field. Gliders. Then a man in a pale blue smock coming in from the side and dismounting his glider. Walking around the field like he was mowing the lawn. Covering every square foot. His motions became jerky as the video fast-forwarded. Then he was gone. Reverse to the man walking. Slow. He's by the tree. He's standing under the branch. He walks forward a couple of steps and . . . disappears!

"He found it," Marco told Dr. Gila. The picture moved back, forward, back, forward. The same thing happened each time. Poof, he was gone. Yellow sent the tube away with a flick of her wrist.

Marco thought the doctor was starting to shift color. He tried to distract her. "Wait a minute," he said. "I have an idea." He realized the genius of it. "I'll go back after him. That makes sense because I know how to get around in 2007, and you all don't. I'll bring him back. He's probably just sightseeing. When I bring him back, you guys tell me how to cure my mom's mental illness and I go home to Riverton and never bother you again. Everybody gets what they want." Marco was very pleased with himself as he watched Dr. Gila confer with Yellow. That good feeling was short-lived.

"Inspector Anole and I agree." Dr. Gila was removing buttons and stick pins from her smock, taking small gadgets out of her pockets, and handing them to the constable, one by one. She turned around so the woman in yellow could inspect her. Yellow nodded and produced a two-inch capsule from her tunic's chest pocket. She twisted it open and withdrew two copper BB things and an inch-long needle. Dr. Gila put one BB in her ear and one in Marco's. It tickled for a second, and then he lost track of it.

"Translators," she said. She lifted the earphone and wire mic from his head and pulled the two buttons from his cheek. She took the needle and pushed it into the soft flesh just below his shoulder. That stung, but when he reached for the wound with his other hand, he couldn't find it.

"Stabilizer," she said. Dr. Gila unfastened her smock and took it off. She stepped out of her skirt and stood under the tree in her pale blue swimsuit. "I'm ready," she said.

"Ready?" Marco asked.

"If it is possible to time travel or shift dimensions, it is very dangerous," Dr. Gila said. "Something from another time or place might seriously alter our future here in 4000. If a person could go back in the past, and somehow affected that world, a killing, or an invention, then the whole future would change from that point on. Novikov's Paradox. Unless there are completely parallel universes. Our science is still some distance from resolving such questions. Right now, I'm guessing nothing bad has happened, because here we are, getting ready to do this. But you may need help with Monitor and I'm in charge of this sector, so I'm coming with you. It's my responsibility."

Marco could sense it wouldn't do any good to argue. Plus, if he decided to, once he got home, he could give her the slip. "Okay," Marco said, "but I wouldn't wear that."

Dr. Gila gave Marco a once-over. "I see what you mean," she said. "I thought your garb was another manifestation of your illness, but if this is a portal, then your outfit is indicative of the primitives."

"I guess you could say that," Marco said, feeling slightly offended.

Dr. Gila put her top and skirt back on. "Does this mark me as a medical in your time?" she asked.

No, Marco thought, it marks you as frumpy, but he didn't say anything. He heard the constable ask the doctor how they would communicate with each other.

"I don't think we'll be able to," Gila replied. "I don't want to take any more of our equipment back into their time, and, besides, I don't think we have anything that would transmit through a wormhole. Please cordon off the park and post a watch, and I'll be back as soon as I can." She touched the middle two fingers of her left hand to the middle of her forehead in what looked like a salute to Yellow and gave Marco a nod, signaling she was ready.

"Uh, my jacket?" Marco felt embarrassed about asking, especially since he had used it to evade the disk, but heck, it was his best jacket, leather and everything.

Gila said something to Yellow that Marco didn't catch. Yellow pulled a cord and whistled into some kind of retractor pin on her lapel. Within a minute, a pale blue tube appeared, escorted by a silver tube. The blue had Marco's coat attached to its flexible arm. Yellow snatched it and handed it to him. When Yellow turned to further instruct the tubes, Dr. Gila turned to Marco.

"Ready now?" she asked.

Marco guessed that he was. They walked into the wavy stuff.

This time when Marco stopped, I opened my eyes right away. I had my questions. But he was just sitting there. Like the Buddha.

"Marco."

He didn't move.

"Marco?"

Nothing.

"Marco, dammit!"

Nothing. His eyes were closed but his posture was straight, chin up, so he wasn't conked out. I reached out to shake him but stopped. What did they say about disturbing a sleepwalker? What if I touched him and he went ballistic? This was all so . . . what if he had gone somewhere in his mind and couldn't come back now?

Strings and
Wormholes

After school the next day, I drove by Marco's house to ask him what he thought he was doing, to confront him. Make him tell me the truth about that story. He wasn't home.

Back at my place, I was sitting in the living room, planning, while Mom was napping in her bedroom. I would wait for midnight, until she was down for the night, and then I'd go motel hunting again. Bars would be closed, and Dad would have sacked for the night. Dad's sneaky but he's lazy. I didn't think he'd be farther than ten miles from the bar where I found him earlier.

I called Hubie, who had most of the same classes I did, to see if I could get some back homework.

"What all have you been doing?" He sounded like he was eating.

"Uh, some family stuff came up and I've been trying to take care of it."

"Your mom again? Tough."

"Hey, could you tell me any homework I missed early in the week?" I didn't want to talk about Mom.

Hubie filled me in.

"If you want to come over, I'll copy the stuff."

"Thanks, but I can't tonight."

"Okay. They'll let you hand them in next week. What else do you have? Chem with Sarah, right? You could call her and she'd tell you the work. Anything else?" he asked.

"History, but we're just reading Zinn and discussing it."

"Cool. Hey, you want to come eat with us?"

"Hey, Hube, I'd like to. Tomorrow maybe."

"Well, if there's anything else you need, call," Hubie said. "You want me to call Sarah about the Chemistry assignments?"

"No thanks. I'll get it later . . . but there is one more thing. Uh, what do you know about wormholes?"

"I thought you only fly-fished."

"No, I mean like in physics. Something that connects two places in space-time? Or even one universe to another?"

"Are you writing a paper of some kind?"

"No. Uh, a friend mentioned the idea, and I wasn't sure I understood about them. Can you . . . could a person go from one time to another, if they found one?"

"Wow. I don't think even Stephen Hawking can answer that question. They're just theoretical, you know. Einstein's relativity, or maybe Witten's string theory, suggests it, I think. And there are a zillion unanswered questions about how they would even work. Like, could information pass through and maintain its integrity?"

"Whoa! Whoa. I just want to know could they jump through time?"

"Well, jump is probably a misnomer."

"Hubie!"

"Okay. Okay. Theoretically, uh, maybe. I have to get through my post-doc at MIT before I can really answer that question."

"Okay," I said, "that's good enough for a start."

"You should be asking Kaitlin about this space stuff," he said. "I think she went lunar several years ago."

Hubie knew I had a thing for his sister. He put up with it. Barely. He never called her Z like she wanted. I bet that made for some fights.

Drug Dealer?

I woke up at the kitchen table about midnight, Trig problems and sheets of scratch paper in a mess around me. I checked on Mom. She was snoring. I wasn't hungry, I wasn't sleepy. I was ready to find Dad.

Before I got in the car, I stood on the porch and closed my eyes, took a deep breath, and tried to get a feeling about where Dad might be, like I had before with the bar. Out of plain sight, I thought, so neither Mom nor Charlene would be likely to run into him. Cheap, but somehow a good deal, like maybe it had refrigerators in the rooms. Close enough so he wouldn't have to drive too far drunk at closing time. He might switch bars since I'd found him, but I didn't think he'd move to a different motel. What was halfway between here and Lake Vista? There were some chains like Budget Lodge on Market Street, north of downtown. They might cut him a deal, like every seventh night free.

I tried those first.

Nothing.

I remembered some cheesy motels on the old highway between Riverton and Lake Vista. His car was parked outside Room 20 in the second one I found, the Eaz-On Inn. I hesitated when I got to the door. What if he wasn't alone? As I stood there, I began to have second thoughts. What if he just agreed to everything I said and then took off again as soon as I wasn't looking? I might not find him next time. I stood outside his door a few seconds longer, thinking, then walked back to my car. Maybe there was a card I hadn't played.

I fell asleep again, trying to finish my homework at the kitchen table. The recycling truck's clanking bottles woke me the next morning. My neck was stiff and I was hungry. I sliced an apple and fixed some cereal. The milk was sour, so I put a couple of spoonfuls of yogurt on the cornflakes. It tasted annoyingly healthy. I added some blackberry jam. I wondered what Hubie was having. And then I wondered about Marco. Had I seen any food in his house?

Mom padded into the kitchen in her pajamas. She looked all wooly, like she had been hibernating.

"You want some yogurt?" I asked.

She stood in front of the refrigerator, not opening it.

"I could make you a sandwich, if you want peanut butter and honey," I said.

She shook her head and walked back down the hall toward the bathroom.

When I heard a door close, I went across the driveway to Mr. Bellarmine's. Why couldn't my dad be more like him?

He opened his door in a blue plaid robe over a white dress shirt, already sort of duded up. "What's happened?" he asked, concern in his voice. "Are you two all right?"

I realized that he knew Dad was gone, though I am sure no one had ever told him. I also realized the recycling truck came around before daylight, and that it must be close to six A.M.

"Yes," I said. "Sure. Don't worry. I, uh, I'm sorry I'm bugging you so early, but I just needed to ask you a favor before I went off to school."

"Do you always make social calls by dawn's early light?" he asked, his eyes quickly making the trip from my hair to my wrinkled clothes.

"No. No, I'm sorry. I just woke up too. I'm going to change clothes," I said, "but I need some help with something later today."

He looked stern but not angry, if that's possible. He nodded.

"That guy you saw . . . the guy who visits?" I tried to keep my voice even, like this was the most normal request in the world. "If you get a chance, would you copy down his license-plate number?"

He cocked her head and squinted at me. Curious.

"Uh, I just want to make sure he's on the up and up. Uh, like with my mom and all."

"You think he's a drug dealer?" he asked.

Sheesh! I hadn't expected him to be so savvy. "I don't know," I said. "Maybe. The thing is, I don't like him here with my mom."

"I agree with your assessment," he said. "Get on to school and I'll set up an observation post."

Walking back to my house, I was trying to remember what work Mr. Bellarmine had retired from. Lawyer? Insurance claims? Whatever it was, it was no-nonsense.

School on Friday was useless. My brain was a cement mixer, Marco-Mom-Dad-Vinnie spinning around in there. I hope I got through the surprise English test fifth period.

First thing after school, I drove by home and checked with Mr. Bellarmine. No license number yet. He had gone grocery shopping and didn't know if Vinnie had come by.

Next, I went by Marco's to make him answer my questions about his story. Nobody home.

Nobody.

What a Party!

When I got back home, I checked on Mom. She was asleep in her bed. The room smelled liked farts and cigarette smoke. I doubted if she'd gotten up or eaten or taken her meds.

I thought about fishing but didn't have the energy and fell asleep in the living room within minutes of turning on some college game on ESPN. I had a dream that I was walking down a school hall, a long school hall, and then the doors and lockers and bulletin boards faded and the hall became darker and smaller, more like a tunnel. Finally I was crawling forward, and it was pitch-black and then it just ended. There I was on my hands and knees in a black tunnel that stopped, and I didn't know if I even had room to turn around.

I awoke feeling churned up, funky, like I had been dragged through dirt back to the surface of the earth. I don't know if it was the dream or what, but I decided I'd get high. Friday night. I wouldn't do that if I was wrestling on the team, but I'd quit, so who cares? Time for the Mander boy to party! By myself. What a party! I stuck Miles Davis's *Kind of Blue* in my stereo and dug out my personal pharmacy: a jay, a mystery pill, and an unopened pint of Jim Beam.

Mom and Vinnie could go screw themselves. Not that they hadn't already. I was pretty sure I knew what he was doing, hanging around her. She was whacked, but she was still pretty. I figured meth and sex. She needed to feel good about herself and, even psychotic, she could get a rush off the powder. Feel high for a while. And he got free sex and a drinking buddy.

I took a long pull off the bottle and it burned. I nearly spit it back up. I wanted to break things! Shoot somebody. Shoot Vinnie. We didn't have a gun in the house. Where could I get a gun?

I decided to pass on the mystery pill. A kid at school had said it was a downer when he gave it to me, but who knew? I fired up the jay and got to work on the Beam. Plenty of benzos in the medicine cabinet if I wanted to get totally subterranean later. Now I was going to slow down a little. Make a careful plan. How'd it go? Revenge is best eaten slow? Something like that. I turned up my tunes, put on my headphones, and got back to the Beam. And my eyes were wet. What the hell was that about?

I woke up Saturday morning thirsty and stinking. The Beam had spilled and I had thrown up sometime during the night. There were flecks of some brown stuff I don't remember eating all over my pillow, on the side of my face, and in my hair.

I tore off the bedding, washed my pillow and mattress with a wet towel, and leaned my mattress against the wall to dry. I scrubbed down my face and hair with a warm washcloth. I couldn't look at myself in the mirror.

There was an inch or so left of the Beam that hadn't spilled out. What do they call that when the sun is already up? A daycap? It was a good start. I didn't want to think what Hubie would say if he saw me right now.

Next time I woke up, I was on my floor with the empty Beam and a battalion of beer bottles. I remembered raiding the fridge before Mom was up. As far as I could tell, she hadn't looked in on me. Good old Ben. Good old stable Ben. Out there taking care of business. Well, adios muchachos, I'm done.

You can't save somebody else.

My room was warm. It felt like early afternoon. I was ready to start a new plan. Okay. Drop school. Stay loaded on summer-job money for a couple of weeks. Then find a studio apartment. Blackmail Dad into rent money or I tell the company that his new office is a bar and he's drinking and drugging his sales into the dust. Then I get a part-time job, I pass the GED, and I start going to junior college. Mom goes down the drain. Nothing I can do about it.

I finish junior college and then . . . then hit the road and never look back. Simple enough. I could do it. I resisted an impulse to pick up an empty beer bottle and throw it at the wall.

Time to get started. No sense overthinking these things. First I would check the fridge and see if I'd left any beer behind. Out in the hall, walking toward the kitchen, I heard voices.

"Put this away," Mom was saying. "Ben'll be home."

"Let him see it." Vinnie's voice. "He knows anyway. You're the adult. You rule."

"No, no," Mom was saying when I walked in the living room. Straws, opened paper bindles, white stuff on a hand mirror. Half-empty six-pack beside them on the coffee table.

"Oh, oooohh." Mom couldn't think what to say to me.

Vinnie stood. "Let's you and me go to the kitchen and talk for a sec," he said, moving past me.

I followed him. When I walked through the kitchen door, he punched me hard in the solar plexus. When I bent over, he kneed me in the head. I went down and skidded on my butt.

I couldn't get any air. I thought maybe he had ruptured something. In a minute I felt something cold dripping on my cheek. When I looked up, Vinnie was holding a wet towel above my head. He let it drop.

"Get yourself together," he said.

While I was mopping blood off my chin and upper lip, he was talking. "Now let's you and me get one thing clear," he said in a strong whisper. "This is your mother's house. She pays the rent and she says what goes. Right now she's saying I'm staying. Got that?"

He toed me with his boot.

"Got that?" he repeated.

I nodded.

"When I'm here, which is once in a while, you're gone." He looked at me real steady to make sure I was paying attention. "Now get out of here. Don't let me see you no more. Clear?"

I nodded.

"And one more thing," he said, burning a hole in me with his eyes. "You keep your mouth shut and maybe I can find a way to keep your mother from getting hurt. Know what I mean, amigo?"

I was starting to space out. Or overload or something. I couldn't seem to track what he wanted me to do.

He toed me again. "Know-what-I-mean?"

"Yeah," I said. My voice was gravelly.

"Clean up the floor and get out of here."

Marco was in his bedroom, asleep in the bag. I shook his shoulder until he sat up. It took a minute for him to come around.

"What happened to you?"

I didn't want to tell him. "Got drunk. Fell," I said. "I want to know about this story you've been telling. How did my mom get in it?"

He raised his eyebrows. Used his fingers to clean out the corners of his eyes. "Look," he said, "I don't know what you're talking about. I'm just telling you what happened to me. I told you it was strange. Take it or leave it."

I was watching his face as he spoke. A crime show I saw said liars look away when they're telling a lie. Sometimes just for an instant. But he was calm. Placid even. Was he on some kind of drug? He didn't seem to be lying, didn't shift his eyes, didn't nod or smile more than usual, didn't get more rigid or more careful.

"Your story has too many coincidences that fit, uh . . ." Suddenly I didn't want to tell him any more. Didn't trust him. Didn't want to give him anything to work with. "Where's your family?" I asked, like maybe if I could keep him off balance, I could get closer to the truth.

He unzipped the sleeping bag and sat on the edge of his bed. "Get a chair," he said.

I didn't move.

"Okay, Dad is traveling, Mom's in the hospital."

"How come you don't have any furniture?"

"I told you, we just moved here. Haven't settled in yet."

"Where did you hear this story?"

He stood. "Look," he said. "You don't want to hear it, don't ask. You want to leave, leave. I'm not coming to your house every day."

How did he know I'd been here every day? He hadn't been home some of the times I'd come by. Was he just guessing? Had he been watching? Oops. I was getting paranoid. Was I going crazy? Was I already there?

I backed off. "Yeah," I said, "you're right. I, uh, I just

wanted to know you better because I had never met another kid with a mentally ill parent. And then you seemed weirded out by what you said had happened to you, and when you told it to me, I guess I got a little upset myself."

"It goes on," he said. "It keeps happening . . . the story."

He left the room and I could hear him in the bathroom. When he came back, he was carrying the chair. "Want to hear more?" he asked.

4000

Dr. Gila held his shoulder so Marco couldn't walk out from the oak tree. She gave a soft whistle.

Marco didn't understand.

She rolled her eyes, held up a single finger.

"One?" Marco whispered. Then it dawned on him. "You mean stop," he said, "wait a minute."

She let go of him and turned to look out through the branches, listening.

Marco bolted, but a blinding pain drove him to his knees before he had taken two steps. The stabilizer! He could feel his shoulder burning. He crawled back to Dr. Gila and the pain receded.

"You and I will search together," she said. "You will guide, and I will think. Are we clear?"

Marco nodded.

"We are in your backyard?" Gila affirmed.

Marco nodded.

"Do not attract attention," Gila warned. "If we encounter someone, you will speak and get them to leave us alone. If you run again, or try to raise an alarm, I will stabilize you back to our time." She paused to see if he understood. "Now, let's go."

Marco's mind was working at hyperspeed on getting away, but for now, he would do as she said.

They left the shelter of the oak tree and surveyed the yard and nearby houses.

"Monitor is a scientist," Gila whispered. "He would be curious and explore, but he would be very careful."

"Would he carry a cloaking device?" Marco asked.

"No. No devices. Too risky. Like Anole and I agreed, only the stabilizer, so we would not lose you, and the translators so we can talk and I can understand the people here. That was unavoidable, but nothing else that would alter history. And I'm sure he would be similarly responsible."

Marco felt his shoulder. It was in there somewhere. Implant.

They went to the back fence and looked over. Nothing. Side fences, nothing. They edged around the house to the shrubbery at the border of the front yard.

"How long has he been here?" Marco wondered.

"A few hours at the most," Gila said.

"Would he have gone inside one of these houses?" Marco asked.

"Doubtful." Gila was holding her fingers to her temples. "He would have been extremely cautious," Gila said. "He was very aware of the risks."

"Marco! Watch out! Another one's behind you!" His neighbor, Mr. Bellarmine, was yelling at him. "Run! Run! I've got 911!"

My neighbor's name is Mr. Bellarmine! I blinked my eyes against a growing headache.

Marco grabbed Gila and pulled her toward his front door. He could feel scales forming on her hand as he reached the steps. Throwing the door open and running inside, he almost ran down his mother, who was standing in the front hallway, facing the door. His mother's face was painted red, and she was holding an odd-shaped cross in front of her. She began screaming. Marco turned to Gila, who was again transforming, her nose blunting, her skin changing texture. He dropped her hand and ran to his mother. The pain dropped him to his knees again. Gila pulled him to his feet and the two of them were outside, running down the block, away from his home and the neighbor with the phone. Marco could feel the scales receding on her hand.

In the middle of the next block, Marco ducked into a yard, pulling Gila toward the back.

"Garvins' garage," he explained, not slowing down. "I do their lawn."

I mow the Garvins' lawn! I swallowed, tasted acid in my mouth.

"They're vacationing," Marco said, letting go of Gila's hand at the garage's side door and pushing hard on the window next to it. A sound froze him. Sirens! He put his weight behind the pushing, and the window opened a crack, then more, then enough for him to squeeze through. The sound was getting louder! Noooo! Not now. He couldn't even imagine what would happen if they were caught. Would the world as he knew it just . . . what? Disappear?

He opened the door from the inside and Gila rushed in. With the slam of the door closing, he bent over, hands on knees, breathing hard. The sirens had gotten very loud and then stopped. What did that mean?

Monitor's voice startled him.

"I don't know how to explain it simply," Monitor said, holding up his hand to ward off their questions. "A sort of time warp, possibly. Inexactitude. Space is not as linear as you might think."

As Gila had earlier, Monitor had taken off his blue smock and was dressed in his swimsuit thing. He was lean and muscular, like an Olympic freestyler, but at the moment, he looked silly standing in a dark garage in his bathing suit.

What was happening with the sirens? Could they have been fire trucks? Marco looked out the side window he had entered but saw nothing except sunlight, trees, and shadows.

Gila had her hands on her hips and looked steamed. She

probably would have said something, but she was still breathing too hard.

"When I came out under the oak tree," Monitor continued, "I knew you had arrived before . . . well, that's not quite true. When your neighbor caught me looking around and began yelling, I ran back to the portal. When I came out on the other side, Anole was standing there with her command tube and I didn't want to get stuck answering to her and lose this opportunity, so I decided to come back here while I still could, and finish what I started."

"What do you mean?" Marco had his breath back. "I started it! I'm the one who told you about it. I want to know how to cure Mom, and you guys are just making it worse!"

Monitor began to get that greenish-bronze hue. Oh jeez!

"Ulrich!" Gila had recovered her breath. "Calm down. Now!"

His coloring receded and his skin resumed its fleshlike texture. What was it? Whenever these guys got excited or upset or . . . or when did she do it the first time? When she made some kind of mind link with what she called the University. Marco wanted to form a theory but clearly didn't have enough information.

"Is this real?" Gila asked Monitor, gesturing to the outdoors.

"That's what I thought at first, too," he said. "That these were all dense holograms, but no, these are actual trees and flowers. Even the buildings in this area are made from genuine natural materials. Must have cost a fortune, yet the people dress very plainly and the tech systems are antediluvian."

* * *

The emotion in Marco's voice rose and fell with the events in the tale like it was a book on tape. How could he know this stuff?

"I told you it's 2007!" Marco said, exasperated at how little respect they seemed to have for his words or his intelligence.

Gila and Monitor looked at each other.

"We have underestimated the boy," Gila said. "He's not nearly as crazy as we thought." Once again she brought her fingers to her temples as if she had a migraine. Or perhaps that helped her think better.

"The garage is surrounded!" A loud megaphone voice coming from the driveway startled the three of them. "Put any weapons down, raise your hands, and walk slowly out the door. Immediately!"

Gila screamed and started to change again.

"Novikov's Paradox!" Monitor swore. "This cannot happen!"

"Come out immediately, hands in the air." The voice was hard, unyielding, an anvil. "We will not negotiate."

Marco jumped into the front seat of the Garvins' Suburban. As usual, the keys were in it. "Get in the back, quick!" he yelled at the two doctors.

The truck started with a rumble, and Marco threw it into reverse, ramming into the closed garage door. The wooden door broke in the middle, sunlight leaked in. In his rearview mirror, Marco saw what looked like a SWAT team.

"Halt! Halt! We will shoot!" The voice was getting even louder.

Marco could see black uniforms, but he wasn't sure

whether the bullhorn man was behind him in the driveway or to the side, near the door they had entered. He jammed the vehicle into four-wheel, slid the automatic tranny into drive, and stomped down on the accelerator. The SUV's tires squealed, and the big machine lurched forward into the plasterboard covering the back of the garage. The wheels smoked, the vehicle hesitated, and then the studs gave way and the truck bulled its way through the wall, snapping siding like kindling. Five or six policemen with guns drawn were stationed around the side yard. All seemed momentarily frozen by the spectacle.

"Don't shoot! Don't shoot!" Marco was screaming, and then they were in the alley and roaring north, back toward Marco's house. He rocketed down the narrow gravel lane, shot across the neighborhood street midblock, and slid to a sideways stop just before his own backyard.

"Come on!" he was yelling, running toward the oak tree, diving under its front branches. Gila and Monitor joined him in less than a second. Lizards both! He grabbed their arms and dragged them with him. Maybe it was the scales. Slippery. Or maybe it was the sweat on his palms, but at the last moment, he lost his grip and fell headfirst into the portal without them.

The silence lasted a long time. Marco was crosslegged on his bed, hands together in front, meditation position again. Daylight let me see him more clearly. He was still wearing the same clothes he had on when I first met him in the admitting lobby. The fleecy vest was pilled up like he had been sleeping in it. His shirt was rumpled. Stains on his pant legs. And he was paler, except around his eyes. His breath was rancid and his hair was dirty. I couldn't fit those facts together with how serene he seemed.

"I do the Garvins' lawn," I said.

He didn't open his eyes.

"Mr. Bellarmine is my neighbor."

He didn't move.

"I'm going to find out what you're doing," I said.

"It's simple," he said, without looking up. "I'm looking for a cure for mental illness."

Did He Hear Me?

I had to get some food in me. I stopped at In-and-Out for a triple burger and then drove to the hospital. I waited in the admitting lobby until a woman, a nurse or mental health worker, opened the unit door and leaned out to see what I wanted.

"I need to speak with Mrs. Lasalle," I told her.

"I'm sorry," she said, "I cannot say who is on the unit and who is not. Are you someone's family member?"

"Uh, yes," I said. "I'm Marco Lasalle, her son."

"No, you're not," she said.

"Wait! Please. Okay, sorry. I'm Ben Mander. My mom

was here for several hours on Tuesday. She must have met Mrs. Lasalle during that time, and I really need to speak to her, just for a second."

"Why don't you wait here," she said, "until one of our staff has a few minutes to talk with you?"

I shook my head.

"I can tell you this," the woman said, "I don't know any Mrs. Lasalle."

The click of the lock echoed in the empty waiting room.

When Mr. Bellarmine opened his front door, he was smiling. Binoculars hung around his neck on a leather strap. He was holding a clipboard in one hand and a chocolate chip cookie in the other. He handed me the cookie.

"Are you on your way out?" I asked, pointing toward the binocs.

"No," he said, "just keeping an eye on the local wildlife." He smiled. "I got it," he said. "7 BBN 219." He pulled a yellow sticky note off the clipboard and handed that to me.

"His license?" I asked.

He nodded. "Black Monte Carlo with those silver wheels."

"Like spinners or mags?"

"Spinners," he confirmed. He looked me over. "Did that man hit you?"

"Him?" I gestured at the car. "No." I didn't want Mr. B. worrying about me. "I got hit with a ball in gym class."

He frowned. "Want to get a restraining order?" he asked.

Dad's car was parked in front of his room at the motel. I thought it might be. Saturdays and Sundays he liked to lay in a supply of beer and watch sports and doze all day long.

It took him a while to answer when I knocked.

"An ex-con is giving Mom speed in exchange for sleeping with her."

"Found me again," Dad said. Flat.

Did he hear me?

"Yeah, I've known where you were for a few days, but I needed to get this last piece of information so you could do something."

"Like what?"

"Track this guy down. Threaten him. Tell the police."

"You want a beer?" he said, opening the door wider.

I could hear a basketball game on the TV. I didn't see anyone behind him in the room. "No," I said. "I don't want a drink, and I don't want to come in. I just want you to do something."

He left the doorway for a moment and came back, handing me two twenty-dollar bills. "Not happening," he said. "Catch you later." He closed the door.

I stood there wondering if I would start the car and drive it into his room.

A Pitch to Team Ludlow

Hubie had a small private space carved out of the flotsam and jetsam in his basement. In the corner farthest from the furnace, he had strung curtains, like screens, made of thin bedspreads. He had a bookcase and stereo on one side, a ratty couch opposite, with an end table and lamp beside it so he could read and relax and listen to music away from the rest of his family. In the middle he had a table and two chairs where we sometimes played chess or, once in a great while, actually did our homework together.

I told him the whole story: Mom, Vinnie, Dad.

"What's the deal with your dad?"

"Dad's, uh, okay, I guess, or he used to be. He'll give me money but he won't help with Mom. I think he's still working but I'm not sure. I don't really think he's a bad guy. He's just selfish and lazy, drinking and using pain meds all the time. Hiding out. Can't cope." Was I defending him too much?

"Well, then, he never should have had any kids!" Hubie said, disgusted.

I wondered if there were a lot of parents like that.

I told him about Marco. Right away his eyebrows went up. Skeptical.

He snorted when I said Dr. Gila's name. "This is a joke, right?"

I felt my face flush. Yeah, they were stupid names. Maybe they were pseudonyms. I don't know. I hadn't given it that much thought, compared to the rest of the story. Other things like the coincidences with my own family had bothered me more. I guess I'd been living with this Lizard stuff too long. Was it a joke? It didn't feel like one. It felt too dumb to be a joke. And Marco didn't seem either brainless or cruel.

"I think you should run this by my mom," Hubie said. "You mind telling her?"

I had to think about that. Why did I keep coming to Hubie's? I coughed, so I had an excuse to turn away for a second. I needed help and I knew it.

"No," I said, my voice scratchy. "Go ahead."

"Another thing," he said. "You're looking pretty gnarly. Before we go upstairs, comb your hair or something."

* * *

His parents were in their living room. His dad was watching some sepia-colored movie on the History Channel and his mom was reading on the couch. I sat on the end away from her. Hubie sat on the floor and leaned against the couch, close enough to hear.

His mom listened without comment, just glanced at me a couple of times during the Vinnie part and the Marco story.

When I stopped talking, Mrs. Ludlow stood and looked me over carefully. I couldn't read her expression.

"Are you okay, Ben?" she asked. Even tone.

I wondered how I seemed to her. "Sure. I mean, I'm probably a little tired, with this stuff and all." I wasn't comfortable with her worrying about me. Huh. Isn't that what I wanted? Isn't that what I came here for?

"You should stay with us for a couple of weeks," she said, reaching out to touch me briefly on the shoulder.

"My mom," I said, shaking my head.

She nodded, understanding. "Let me think about your mom," she said.

"We're supposed to be getting help from a county caseworker, but I haven't seen her," I said.

"Who?" she asked.

"Betty Lou somebody."

She nodded again, like she knew the woman. "This Marco, what do you know about him for sure?"

"He lives in a house across the freeway, on the northeast side. His mom was on the unit at the same time as my mom. That's where I met him," I said. "In the lobby, uh, the admitting area. I tried to ask about his mom at the unit today, but they wouldn't tell me anything."

"Honey, does Winona still work in the psychiatric hospital?" she asked Mr. Ludlow.

He shrugged. Went back to watching his program.

"Tomorrow, I'll make some calls," she said. "I went to nursing school with Winona." She rubbed her chin with the knuckle of her thumb. Thinking. "Might even check in with Mrs. Swenson, Betty Lou, with your permission."

She looked at me. "How about having a snack and sleeping here tonight?" she asked again. She glanced at my clothes. "Want me to do some laundry for you and your mom?"

I said no and thanked her. Told her I sincerely appreciated her help. Said I'd come by tomorrow afternoon and visit, but that I needed to get home and make sure everything was okay.

When I headed out, I saw that Z was standing just inside their front door.

"I'll walk you to your car."

"I didn't drive," I told her.

"I'll walk you to the street."

When we got to the sidewalk, she said, "Seems like things might be getting a little trippy."

"Yeah, well, you know. A lot going on. But hey, how are you doing? You're looking really great today."

She was. Short black dress, blood-red scarf around her hips, high-top Doc Martens, white Laplander cap with a red snowflake design.

I smiled.

She didn't. She didn't say anything. Rubbed one hand with the other. Looked at me. Took her bottom lip between her teeth.

I was happy just standing there, looking at her.

"Hulk Human," she said, like Hulk Hogan, but not in her usual teasing voice. "You're looking a little raggedy. Things taking a toll? Who hurt you?"

"Yeah," I said, "physically or mentally?"

She waited me out.

"Well, I got to me first by drinking a hole in my brain."

She nodded, silent.

"Then Mom's new crackster boyfriend busted me up a little. I'm working on getting rid of him." Should I keep going? "Uh, Dad pretty much wrote me off. He's definitely not going to help me with Mom."

I decided not to mention Marco's story. What if she laughed? Worse, what if she thought . . . "I don't know," I finished, "things just seem so crazy sometimes. You know?"

She reached out and touched my elbow for a second or two. "You tell me if things get stranger," she said.

My home was quiet. Living room cleaned up. Mom in bed. Alone. I tried not to make any noise as I bagged the bottles in my room and took them outside to the recycling bin.

In the bathroom I saw myself in the mirror. I didn't look like a wrestler. Or a fisherman. Or a student. I looked more like a cadaver. Night of the Living Teenager.

Betty Lou Weighs In

The doorbell rang while I was rummaging in the fridge for breakfast.

"Betty Lou! What are you doing here? It's Sunday. Where were you all week?"

"Which question do you want me to answer first— Ben, isn't it? Yes, well, I've come by Wednesday, Thursday, and Friday afternoons, knocked till I have calluses, and nobody's come to the door. Your mom still here?"

"Yeah, uh, yes. I've been at school a lot. I don't know why nobody let you in. Mom pretty much stays in her room."

"So, how's your mother doing?"

"Not too well, it doesn't seem like. A guy's been spending time with her. Giving her drugs, meth or coke, I think."

"Son, you can't let that happen!"

"I tried to stop it. He hit me. I think he's an ex-con."

"Well, let's get rid of that piece of garbage. Your mom home now?"

"I think so. Get rid of him how?"

"Why do you think he's a con?"

"He's got those tattoos all down each arm."

"Sleeves," she said. "They call them prison sleeves."

"He has these scars on his face, like from fighting. Bad teeth. He talks like a punk, makes threats."

"That describes a lot of the people I work with. Is he buff? Has he been lifting?"

"No. He's got a pot gut. But he's mean."

"I'll check him out. What's his name?"

"Mom calls him Vinnie. I really only have his car license."

"Are you sure it's his car?"

That question deflated me. "No."

"You told Dullborne?"

"Not yet."

"When does the guy come around?"

"Midday, I think. Stays awhile. He may be kind of like Mom's new boyfriend."

"Oh, for Sam Hill! No wonder they didn't let me in. Well, write his license down. I'm going to go see your mother."

I watched her walk past. She was way overweight, had a limp, looked at least seventy. Seemed like she wore black pants, white shirt, and the same black tennies whenever she worked, even if it was on a weekend. Something my dad used to say came to mind: "Tough old bird." I wrote down the license number and waited for her in the living room.

When she came out, she had a grim look on her face. "She's only been taking about half of her meds. You know that?"

I shook my head.

"She's doubled or tripled up on her benzos. I think that's why she hasn't erupted yet. Can't anyone see that she takes her pills right?"

"I'm at school. What do you expect?"

"You're seventeen?"

I nodded.

"That's too old. Child Protective won't pull you out. They got their hands full with younger kids. Hell of a situation." She paused like she was thinking. Tugged at her pants, tucked the back of her shirt in. "Looks like I'm the best you got. Get me that license and I'll get hold of Dull. Maybe he can do something from his end."

She left while I was still thinking that over. She calls him Dull? To his face?

I went to the neighborhood market and got some milk and cereal and bananas, yogurt and pudding, ready-made coleslaw, seedless grapes.

What's Mom been eating? I felt like she lived on another planet. I couldn't picture her daily routine, any more than I could picture the inside of her mind. She probably slept or watched TV or did whatever Vinnie suggested when he visited.

Putting the stuff in the fridge, I saw the phone message light was blinking.

"Call me." Betty Lou's voice.

When I called, she picked up on the first ring.

"His last name's Rupert."

"Vinnie?"

"It's Elvin Rupert. Vinnie, Elvin. He's out on parole. Dullborne's going to pay him a visit. You stay out of his way. Rupert's, that is. Completely away from him. Got me?"

Around noon I was back at Marco's. He was in his room on his bed fast-forwarding through what looked like a new *Time* magazine.

"Where's your mom?"

He raised his shoulders, like, Why ask me?

He closed the mag and pushed himself back against the wall. Assumed the zenny position. "Next installment?" he asked.

I had brought the dining room chair in with me.

4000?

Marco stumbled out onto the grass into the sunshine of a warm afternoon. The projected cedar was missing but there were a variety of other trees. He touched the nearest one. Real! He grabbed a low limb and climbed to survey the situation. There was no sign of Anole. Still, this could be the same park as before. The paths were different, cobblestone with flowers bordering. Marco saw people were walking instead of gliding. No tubes were visible.

"Why always the third person?" I interrupted. Watching Marco's face.

He stopped speaking for a minute. Looked up at me. "It's how it comes to me," he said.

"Comes to you? Like in a trance or like channeling?"

"It's how I go back and forth," he said. "Otherwise I can't make it real."

Yeah, it's not real. It couldn't be.

He took a couple of deep breaths, closed his eyes, and started speaking again.

Marco climbed down and approached the nearest walker, a slender person with very short brown hair. No swimsuits anymore. Some kind of opaque gossamer robe, loose fitting.

The walker turned as he approached, and raised her eyebrows. "Marco?" she asked. "How remarkable that I should be the one to see you!"

Marco couldn't think of anything to say. How did this person know his name?

"Of course, you must be surprised," the walker filled in, "but we've been expecting you for years. Who is it you wish to speak with first? The Venerable Gila? The Venerable Monitor? I'm Sauria, and I'm a follower of Inspector Anole, but I don't believe you knew her as well."

"Inspector Anole?" Marco repeated, struggling to catch up.

"Anole, founder of the new technocracy. Aren't the differences wonderful? Miniaturization? No need for those wires or the tubes or any of the old equipment. Haven't had them for years."

Marco realized he was able to understand the walker's speech without the translator wires.

"As soon as I recognized you, I alerted the grid. I'll show you. Try to back up."

Marco attempted to step away but was unable to move in any direction.

"Please don't be upset. The Venerable Gila knew it would take time for you to adjust, no matter when you returned, so plans for your reception have been in place for years."

"What year is it?" Marco asked, growing increasingly alarmed.

"4030. Please don't worry." The walker put the middle two fingers of her left hand to the center of her forehead, like Gila had done earlier. "We are at your service, and you will be free to move about at your discretion, as soon as the Venerable Ones have spoken with you.

"Look." The walker made a sweeping gesture with her hand. "Isn't it beautiful? All these trees, the stone glide paths, the flowers. All these are the work of the Venerable Monitor, the founder of naturalism. So much has changed, thanks to you!"

Marco was again at a loss for words.

"Do you notice the excitement in my voice? A broad range of expression is now encouraged in our culture. For hundreds of years, emotionalism was biochemically dampened to discourage the furtherance of classism, nationalism, and war. Now we are free to bloom again, like our flowers."

"What happened?"

"That is not really mine to tell you," the girl said, blushing. "I have probably already spoiled some of their surprises. But I don't think Venerable Gila will mind, Though she is not my primary, I thank her daily for my liberation. Her founding of Emofirst has given us all richer lives."

Marco was feeling a pressure to move to his right. He found himself resisting, not only because he didn't know what was causing this pressure, but also because he was interested in this girl and her explanations, and he was reluctant to leave her.

The pressure was not painful, but it was strong enough to push him into a step and then another and another to keep himself from falling.

"Will you come with me?" he asked, looking over his shoulder as he moved away. "Can you?" he yelled back at her.

He could see her smile as he was herded by the constant pressure toward the boulevard at the edge of the park. Did she even hear him?

The pressure stopped at an access to the stone path. A stone at the edge lifted to hip height. The top half opened like a lid and showed a blue LED screen and a keypad. Something, possibly a remote from some other location, typed onto the screen. The writing was similar to before, lines, dashes, and dots. No translation was provided. The lid closed and the stone returned to the ground, nestling unobtrusively among the others.

Marco felt a pressure to move forward onto the path. As he did, he found himself flowing—was that the right word?—to the right, toward buildings that looked like those he had seen before. When he reached the street, he felt himself gently turned and propelled along the street in the direction he remembered. He wasn't moving his feet but he was . . . gliding along without standing on anything he could see. Was this part of Inspector Anole's new technocracy?

At a rose-tinted building shaped like an enormous stylized teardrop, he was gently edged off the street and moved to the entrance, where a panel opened and he continued to be guided inside. When the panel closed behind him, an opaque shield in front of him lifted. Standing only a few feet beyond it was a group of people in glittering metallic-colored clothes: coppery blues, bronzes, subtle greens. In front of the group stood three people Marco recognized. Monitor, Gila, and Inspector Anole. They were smiling and posed in that fingers-to-middle-forehead salute position. When the shield was fully opened, they released their salute and stepped forward.

Marco tried to step back, instinctively wanting more space until he could figure out what was happening. Whatever it was wouldn't let him.

"Let us welcome you appropriately this time." Gila was the first to speak.

Marco wondered if this was some kind of elaborate trick.

"Your bravery has brought forth a renaissance." Monitor said.

Anole stepped forward, closing the small distance, and reached toward him.

Marco flinched but could not retreat or duck to avoid her touch.

Using one of her finger rings, she gently extracted the stabilizer from his shoulder.

He had totally forgotten about it! But he quickly found he still couldn't move. Miniaturization, he remembered.

She stepped back to stand with the others.

"There is so much to tell you," Gila said, "so much gratitude to convey, so much to share with you. Please come with us and let us start."

The lobby, or whatever it was, was filled with humming and clicking.

It was a pleasant sound. Maybe it was applause.

There was a very brief ceremony right there in front of the small crowd of people who wore stripes and medals and looked like officials of some kind. Marco smiled to cover his confusion. After he had been thoroughly greeted, Anole, Gila, and Monitor escorted him in a glass elevator to the second level, an open area that looked like a pie cut into thirds. There was a central desk or reception area, and a broad hall going off in each direction. A mercury-colored symbol hung above each entrance.

Inspector Anole stepped forward again. Took Marco's arm. Gently. "Why don't you come with me first?" she asked him, but she was looking at the other two.

He could see they agreed.

"Whenever you're ready, I'll be in my office," Monitor said.

"Likewise," Gila said, "and I'll wait as late as necessary." She smiled.

Inspector Anole led him down the leftmost of the three corridors.

Her corner office was huge, the outdoor walls all windows. A big woman needed a big office, Marco guessed. In the middle was a thick, many-colored carpet with cushioned chairs around the edge. When Anole pointed, two of the chairs moved to the center of the carpet, facing the windows, talking-distance apart. Every gesture seemed theatrical, grand, as if the constable had grown an ego to match her height and girth.

"As you can see," she said, "everything now follows the discovery you facilitated. Every design is subservient to natural beauty and the state of Flow that it engenders. Transportation, security devices, communication aids are all either invisible or cloaked. In daily living, we wish to have our observations be informed by aesthetics, not distracted by machinery. Form follows nature, or vanishes! Is our world not a great deal more beautiful in just thirty years?"

Of course, it was still the very same week to Marco, but he didn't tell her that. He wondered if she had already planted more invisible controllers on him when she touched him earlier.

"All is possible, young man," she said, smiling. "With Fusion, all is possible."

Deep Ancestral DNA

"**Marco,** Marco, Marco," Monitor was smiling broadly, expansive, but he remained seated behind a console that actually seemed to be growing its own leaves. "The man of the century," he said, clasping his hands and smiling. "It may be hard for you to believe that we had completely eschewed nature by the year 4000. By 2800, of course, we, mankind, had not only conquered nature, but eliminated most of it. Natural gas, petroleum, even aquifers had been gone for at least two hundred years. The greenhouse effect and global warming had made weather hopelessly chaotic and completely unmanageable. After the ozone disintegration, we had to keep our heads down, so to speak, until we were able to artificially re-constitute a UV absorption screen. Even so, everyone's skin darkened. The remaining bits of nature, plants and the like, seemed troublesome since we manufactured our own oxy-gen and no longer needed their contribution. We had a holo-graphic record of pretty much every living thing since the twenty-fifth century, so we simply projected the nature we wanted, clouds, trees, and so on. Never have to prune a holo-gram," he said, chuckling.

"It took our trip to your time to show me what we were missing. The smell, the textures, the variation, the entire liv-ing process. Inspiring really."

Dr. Gila was standing in her familiar pose, hands together in front of her. Her office, like the other two, was very large and full of sunlight. Is it really sunlight? Marco wondered. Along with the two walls of glass, there was a wall of cacti, many in bloom, blood-orange knobs and deep red fluted stalks leaning out over the spines.

"Now, the least we can do is answer your questions," Gila said, "and I believe the first had to do with a cure for mental illness?"

"Yeah," Marco said, "and the University. What's the Uni-versity? And the Lizard thing. What is going on with the Lizard thing?"

"Actually your last question is the easiest," Gila said, look-ing out the window, as if the answer were inscribed on a cloud. "Emotions are primary. They override cognition and reason. In 4000, we were all taking supplements that assisted in the suppression of feelings. When we had to use extrasensory communication, that particular neural configuration brought a flood of emotions to the surface, different than, but similar in effect to, adrenaline. Fight or flight. The emotional brain, the reptilian brain, the primitive brain, would break through. The unfortunate side effect of reengineering and suppressant use was that, with the emotional breakthrough, inevitably came a momentary swelling, plus pigmentation and skin configuration disruption. As you saw, for seconds at a time, we began reverting to very deep ancestral DNA."

I got up so fast my chair went over backward. I wanted to throw something. Why was he laying this on me? Maybe I'd been wrong. Maybe he was cruel. Crazy. Into some ugly mind game. I couldn't figure out what to do. Marco stayed as still as a rock. After a minute, Mrs. Onabi flashed in my mind. *Get back to class.*

I righted my chair and sat.

"As to the University, the University is the governing body that controls the supplements, provides the genetic engineering, and conducts the experiments that inform future decisions regarding our species' psycho-physiological structuring. Thanks to you, as the creator of Emofirst, I am now president of that University.

"And your last question . . . sadly, I can give you very little to cure mental illness in 2007. You do not yet have the neuropsychological inventions to change the nature of illness, and your epoch's government lacks compassion for social support. Families in your time are left to fend for themselves."

*　　*　　*

I didn't realize the yelling was mine. I knew the rage was. I stomped out to the dining room.

When I pulled myself together, Marco was gone.

I walked through his house looking for him. Like before, no furniture, no people. But I realized something else. No parents' bedroom. No bed. No dressers. His mom's a decorator? No way. No tools, no books, no . . . I went to every small room and checked every closet. No clothes. Kitchen? Cabinets empty.

Nobody's living here. Marco sleeps here.

Maybe.

Take-Down

Driving home, the sadness left me but the rage stayed. I thought about going fishing for an hour or so to settle down, but I was too restless.

My wrestling coach always said, "Never get mad in a match. All the blood goes to your arms and legs." It leaves your brain, in other words, and you get stupid and make a mistake, and then you're upside down on your shoulders and the ref is counting you out.

It took running a stop sign to wake me up, and then some deep breathing to calm me down. It would have worked, too, if the Monte Carlo hadn't been parked in front of my house.

Vinnie was there on the couch with Mom when I walked in our front door. He stood and stepped out from the coffee table, and I hit him with a running tackle, butting him in the solar plexus, and we slid together across the wood floor into the bottom of the recliner Dad used to sit in. While he was gasping for breath, I hit him in the ear. I knew that hurt. I'd had it happen to me. I found the knife he carried in a Kevlar sheath on his belt, and put it in my pocket and stood up. He was curled up. I stomped on his foot. I don't think I broke it, but his groaning got louder. He would have yelled if he'd had any breath. I grabbed him by the collar and dragged him across the wood floor toward the front door. Did he have a gun in his car? Could I find it if he did?

The doorbell rang. Geez, what was Betty Lou going to think?

But it wasn't Betty Lou. It was Man-mountain Dullborne.

He looked down at Vinnie, then back at me. "Looks like you've apprehended a parole violator," he said, pulling the handcuffs off his belt.

Now I could hear Mom screaming. I'd forgotten all about Mom. Sounded like she'd gone back to her bedroom.

I heard Dullborne yell, "I'll put him in the car and be back!" I shouldered open Mom's door, realizing at the last millisecond that she might be behind it. She wasn't. She was standing on her bed, with her arms out like wings, making a terrible sound. Her face was twisted by the noise she made, her teeth were bared, and her eyes were volcanic.

I began talking to her softly, wondering if she could even hear my voice over the sound of her tantrum. I held my hands out, fingers down, disarmed. I was saying, "Easy, Mom, easy, it's going to be okay."

I got to the side of the bed and looked around to see whether there was anything Mom could grab and swing at me if I reached out for her. She was breathing so hard her chest was rattling.

I snuck up behind her and hugged her tight, hoping that would help her get control of herself. "I love you, Mom," I was whispering. "Don't cry!"

Was that what Mom was doing? Was that crying? She sounded like Jurassic Park.

"Take it easy, Mrs. Mander," Officer Dullborne said from behind me. "We're all going to stay right here and make sure you're safe."

I don't know if it was my hugging or Dullborne's words, but Mom stopped screeching.

In a few minutes, she was willing to let me give her a Klonopin. She lay down and told us to leave her alone. Whatever force had animated her was gone. She looked completely exhausted, could hardly hold her eyes open. Officer Dullborne and I went to the living room.

He took rubber gloves from a pouch on his belt and stretched them onto his hands. He produced a resealable plastic bag from another pouch and swept the mirror and blade and powder off the coffee table into it.

"Can Vinnie, uh, Rupert, get out?" I was coming down from the anger and feeling wiped out and more than a little worried.

"No," Dullborne said. "It's a cage car, like a mini-jail. But I'm going to check on him right now to make sure he's conscious. I need to get him to the hospital. We've had some of these meth guys die after using and fighting. Heart gives out."

"Are you going to release him soon?" I thought Vinnie might shoot me or . . . I didn't want to think about it.

"Nope. He's down for a stretch. Solid time. Years. Breaking parole with drugs, plus whatever he has in his ride . . . likely a gun, there or in his crib."

That reminded me. I handed over the knife.

Dullborne bagged it. "Running his name, I saw he's wanted in Oakland for popping two guys over a dope burn. South Bay wants him for questioning on an armed robbery. He goes back for the five years left on his sentence, and the Oakland thing would be his third strike. Years and years. Where'd your mom meet him, anyway?"

I didn't know, but I had to wonder if he had spotted her somehow at Mental Health and thought she would be easy pickings.

Calls and Whimpers

I had already decided I would skip school until I got things worked out here at home. Getting Vinnie out of the mix gave me new resolve. I stayed home that night and made sure Mom took her evening meds right. Mom looked exhausted, probably coming down from the meth, along with the extra benzos, or maybe she was just wiped from all the excitement. I was upset and restless, but I made myself fix us some sandwiches for dinner and got Mom to sit with me while I watched TV, until she conked out sometime around midnight.

The next morning I left a message for Betty Lou

telling her we needed a family conference and asking if she could stop by right away. I knew she had fifty or a hundred other clients, or more. I hoped she could make it soon, but no matter, I was going to stay home as long as it took to make a workable plan.

Betty Lou called back and said she'd be by in the late afternoon and for me to phone every relative I knew about and see whether any would be willing to take care of Mom for a few months, like you would do for an ailing father or mother.

I started with Mom's two sisters in Utah. They each said no right off.

I remember Mom saying her half brother and his wife in Manteca were "do-gooders." I should have started with them. He, Arvin, said yes after a fairly bad argument with his wife, most of which I caught over the phone. If I heard right, the promise of a new car and some remodeling swung the deal. I had never met him or his wife, and I did my best to prepare them for how Mom was. He said he didn't think it would be an impossible problem because his wife was very involved in the temple, and she and her friends were always looking for a project that would help someone.

By noon Mom was up and in the kitchen, eating some toast and drinking fruit juice. I told her we were going to have a family meeting later today, and that I'd wake her if she was asleep. She avoided my eyes. I thought I heard her say, "I'm sorry," as she shuffled back to her bedroom.

*   *   *

When Betty Lou came, I gave her the half brother's name, address, and phone number.

"Isn't your mother still married?" she asked.

"Yeah, to Dad, but I don't think he'll mind."

"He won't interfere with this plan?" she asked, watching me closely to see if I was pulling a fast one.

"Dad?" I may have snorted. "He took himself out of the equation a few months ago. He gives me money, but he said he's never coming home again. He kind of washed his hands of the whole problem."

"Well, he didn't get them very clean, did he?" Betty Lou said, frowning.

I hated to think it, but I was ashamed of my dad. Ashamed that Betty Lou knew what a loser he was. And I wondered if I would ever forgive him. But I didn't say that.

"Well, I think he's maybe got his own problems," I said, instead. "He's done a disappearing act, but he's not really nasty. He's just . . . he just won't be involved."

"He has to be involved enough to write you a note to school explaining your absences," Betty Lou said, covering the bases. "Got to get the school thing square or the whole plan could cave in."

"Right. I'll get Dad to write a note." *Screw him, Z will do it.*

I brought Mom to join Betty Lou and me in the living room. They sat. I stood.

"I called this," I said, holding Mom's attention with

my look, "because I can't do this family thing anymore. I have to go to school and have a life of my own. I can't stay home and take care of you, and right now, you can't take care of yourself. Betty Lou is going to help you get settled with Arvin in Manteca."

Mom groaned and rolled her eyes. "Ohhhhh," she said, like a wail. "Ben . . . I can't go there. What will they think of me?" She started crying.

Betty Lou said, "Mrs. Mander," but I interrupted her.

"Mom, you've got to think about what's best for me, too. I can't take care of you here, and you won't take care of yourself. And you need people your own age who can make sure you take your medication like you're supposed to. I can't help you, but Arvin and his wife can, and that's the way it's going to be."

Mom whimpered but didn't say any more. After maybe twenty seconds of silence, she started crying again.

"So, when does this all start?" I asked Betty Lou.

"Wait a minute," Betty Lou said, wincing like she was annoyed. "What about you? You're a minor. I can't knowingly make a plan that will leave you home alone with no supervision."

"Well," I said, thinking as I spoke, "I'm, uh, I have a family that will watch over me until I am eighteen. I just have to make a call to set it up."

Mom's crying got louder.

"So, when does this start?" I asked Betty Lou again.

"Best case scenario, five to ten days for your mom. That is, if you or your family transports her. I can make the clinical transfer to San Joaquin County so they'll be ready to monitor your mom's condition and provide her medications."

When Betty Lou left, it was dusk and our house was pretty somber. We hadn't turned any lights on. Mom and I sat together in the living room, leaning against each other on the couch. Mom was dozing. I was looking out the window, watching neighborhood kids ride their bikes and goof around until they got called home for dinner. An evening with the Manders, before they go to their placements.

I could picture Hubie saying, "Don't worry. Years from now you'll look back on these touching, fond family moments . . . and run away crying and screaming." Right. Actually, this was the most peaceful time we had spent together in months.

I had trouble sleeping that night. Partly because I was excited about the changes that would be happening, but mostly because I couldn't get Marco out of my mind. Who was he? What was going on with that story? How could he know those details about my life, my mom's delusions, my neighborhood? Sometime after three in the morning, I got dressed and drove to his house.

The front door was unlocked. That was a little surprising. But I guess Marco thought there was nothing much to steal. I tried the lights but none of them would come on. That was peculiar. Made the house kind of eerie. The three straight-backed chairs were in a semicircle, facing each other in the nightglow by the large dining room window. Like someone had been sitting in them, talking in the dark so they wouldn't be seen by any neighbors.

The kitchen remained empty, unused, no glasses or plates. Bathroom: no towels. No toilet paper! Nothing in any other room except Marco's. And there, his bed made, sleeping bag zipped. The whole house was silent, dusty like the carpet hadn't been vacuumed for months. A vague smudge of footprints from the front door to Marco's room. And maybe some marks by the chairs.

I noticed a wadded-up piece of paper under the chair nearest the dining room window. I picked it up. Not paper. Maybe a thin but stiff kind of cloth or plastic. When I spread it out, it had some lines and dots on it like a code of some sort. I couldn't read it. Tossed it back on the floor.

I went back into his room. Felt like I should be tiptoeing. I could smell his sleeping bag. Sour. It needed to be aired out. Through his window I thought I could see, back at the far end of his yard, the large dome-shape of an oak tree, branches moving quietly in the night breeze.

Z!

The best thing that happened during the next two weeks was Z's unexpected visit. I got as close as I'll probably ever get to dating Z.

A couple of days before, Betty Lou had asked me if Mom "cheeked" her medicine, pretended to take it but really not. When I said I didn't know, Betty Lou told me to give it to her and watch her swallow it, and then ask her to open her mouth real wide immediately to make sure it had disappeared. Betty Lou said it would be embarrassing at first, but then it would begin to get routine, and this would make sure Mom got thinking clearer.

Anyway, Mom was fed, med, and off to bed. I was getting ready to visit Marco, when I heard a horn honking out front. Vinnie? I grabbed an umbrella from a stand by the front door. Mary Poppins meets Godzilla.

Z! In her beater that might have originally been a Honda. Waving me over while she stayed in the driver's seat.

"Onetime, no-frills offer," she said, through the rolled-down passenger window. "I'm off to a party. Thought you might want to join me."

"A party," I said.

"Very good," she said. "You're able to repeat in English. Of course, statistics show that most crimes are committed by repeaters."

"No," I said, trying to collect myself. "I'd like to go out with you. I, I'm just not ready or anything."

"Let's be clear," she said. "I am practically a junior in college. I've got about four years on you. You're jailbait. You are not 'going out' with me. You are riding with me to a function. We're . . . acquaintances. This is not a date. Comprendez vous?"

Whatever! "Do I need a coat?" I wondered if my breath smelled.

"Yeah, and a haircut, and probably a steam bath, but get a jacket and let's roll. Carry some change. There could be a cover."

I brushed my teeth, pulled on a clean sweatshirt, and grabbed my good leather jacket. If this was social work, bring it on!

*　*　*

I had imagined the teen club that's always changing hands down by the Liquor Barn. Or even the sports bar over by the new post office. Not to be. We headed west on 299 to the Whiskeytown Overlook and took the road south toward the dam. Brandy Creek Beach? Nope. We didn't take the cutoff over the dam, went straight instead, and wound up at the old cemetery. I could hear a mishmash of music from the far side of the graveyard and see what looked like flickering candles illuminating moving bodies. Live bodies, I was hoping. We sat for a minute in the parking lot while Z looked around. Then she drove a quarter mile or so to a trailhead parking lot and turned off the car.

"The greenies come, we may have to circle back here away from the road," she said. She got out and wrapped a long black shawl painted with bright yellow skulls over her black T-shirt and red plaid jeans.

The greenies? . . . Park Rangers?

From the backseat she grabbed a necklace made out of rubber costume store rattlesnakes woven together, and put it around her neck outside the shawl. She made sure her combat boots were tied, and finally, she ran her fingers along her sideburns, the only hair that wasn't spiked for tonight's spookfest. Her face was glow-in-the-dark white, her lips black. I looked down at my wrestling sweatshirt and blue jeans. Hmmm.

"We'll walk the road, but if a car comes by, step behind a tree. We'll probably see the Rangers' strobe lights before we have to jam," she said. "I won't leave without you."

I nodded.

"Until then, raise hell and no puking." She snake-danced away toward a knot of people with multicolored hair and enough metal on their faces to pick up a Chicago radio station.

My eyes were adjusted to the dark and stayed that way unless I looked directly at one of the big black cylinder candles. Or I guess they weren't all black. Some were red. Looked like they were homemade in gallon coffee cans. Decent light and pretty safe in the winter woods. There was no moon, but occasionally stars shone through broken clouds and pine limbs.

There was a tub—a trough? People were dipping cups in it, and I could make out empty bottles lying beside it. Vodka, tequila, Mountain Dew, and something with Asian characters on the label. I picked it up. It smelled like brake fluid.

"Quaff it, Chip."

A wiry guy in a baseball uniform, battered Uggs, and a blue bus driver's hat was standing beside me, waving his empty cup. I left him and went looking for a beer that hadn't been opened. Surely these folks also drink beer?

"Hey, Z tells me you're a mere child. Let me be maternal."

This from a girl or young woman wearing what looked like silver underwear over black mechanic's coveralls. She had an inch or two of height on me, a smile that showed a split between her front teeth, and crimson lipstick that was smeared just enough to remind me of my mother. *No way.*

I shook her hand like I was an imbecile and fled without speaking. Near the cemetery fence, I fell in with a tangle of party animals dancing together to a boom box barely visible in the middle of their group amoeba. I squished in.

"Watch my toes," a possibly attractive girl warned me. She didn't look old enough to be in college. For some reason, she had covered her face in black dots.

"Will do," I said, waiting for the next time she was facing my direction. "My name's Ben."

"Ben," she said, like she was tasting it. "Sounds trashy."

"Funny, luv!" said a heavyset guy beside her. He was bulging in an orange hoodie and orange workout pants, with a piece of black garden hose hanging down behind him like a tail. "Trash *bin!* Good one!"

"Ben," she said again, continuing to turn and bump. "Franklin?" she asked, facing Orange Guy, instead of me. "You should be high as a kite."

This wasn't going anywhere I wanted. I extricated myself from the body blend and looked for Z. Edging along the fence, I kicked something that clanked. Bottles. A cooler. Beer!

"Dollar a bottle, you want one." A blondish smooth-faced guy in a sportcoat stopped dancing and walked over to me. Was that a costume, or was he a bank trainee in real life?

"First-timer?" he asked.

I ignored that. "Ben," I said, meeting his hand for a quick shake. "Yeah, I'd like two."

The light in that spot was very dim, but he reminded

me of somebody. I couldn't think who . . . Marco? I shook off that thought. No Marco tonight!

He dug under the ice and handed me the two beers as he pocketed my bills.

"Whose party is this?" I asked him.

He smiled. "Not sure, really," he said. "You just got to know somebody who's clued where it's going to be. I'm one, but you don't know me, so that won't work."

"What's your work?" I asked him. Curious if I was right.

"University," he said. "Admissions," dancing back to join his group.

I went off to find Z. It wasn't easy because everybody stayed pretty close together, even if they were in separate little groups. I found her on the right fringe, doing some kind of alien tango, clamped tightly to two other people, no music. The three of them collapsed to the ground, laughing.

"What was that called?" I asked her when she stood again. I handed her a beer.

"Thanks," she said, giving me a look like I was actually a friend instead of a chore. "I don't know," she said, giving a mini-shrug. "The Bango Fandango?"

Her friends were still on the ground, snuggling and giggling.

She saw me watching them. "Hey," she said, "want to fox-trot?"

"I don't know how foxes trot," I said, still sober but feeling giddy.

"Well," she said, "I think in eighth grade they taught

you how boxes waltz." She grabbed my beerless hand, stepped into me, and began leading.

I never would have imagined the waltz could feel so good.

I saw the multicolored lights flipping through the trees before I heard the burst of a siren. Z grabbed my hand and we bushwhacked back to the trailhead and got in her car. Listened to her CDs on the way home, while I tried to think of something to say to her.

She stopped in front of my house and smiled at me, and then she was all business. "Might want to shower before you go to bed," she said. "Lot of poison oak out there."

"Hey, uh, thanks for thinking of me. I really . . . that was great." I wanted to kiss her hand or her cheek or something, but I didn't. She might have hit me. I just got out and stood at the curb.

My block was dark and quiet. Somewhere way behind me, a dog barked once. The air was chill and clean and full of the peppery trace of neighborhood spruce trees. I watched her taillights make their way down my street until they blinked one last time and were gone.

Lizard History

One evening, I think to make contact, to get some kind of response, I did something the doctors said I should never do. I asked Mom about the Lizard People.

Her eyes came up to mine as soon as I said it. Watching. To see if I was serious.

I nodded. Once. Unsure.

She looked off to the side and then closed her eyes.

"They're real," she said. "No one knows where they came from. They were the earliest Indians, before the Anasazi, but they were Lizards and they had to live below the surface. They built big underground cities, a labyrinth in the Los Angeles . . ." She opened her eyes and looked at me again. Was I listening? Was this a trick? Did I believe her?

I met her gaze and stayed absolutely still. I had not heard so much strength in her voice for weeks.

She closed her eyes again.

Did that help her keep the lid on?

"Four thousand years ago," she said, "the Hopi Indians . . . a chief told his tribe about the Lizard People. They were all part of the before time. The Lizard People built these cities to protect against a big fire, like, uh, missiles, er, media showers—"

"Meteor showers?"

She didn't pause. "Meteor showers, and they ruined the crops and killed everybody, but the Lizards were down in these caves they built, so they were safe. Most of them, for a while. Well"—she glanced at me to see if I was following her—"they're coming back now. Up to the surface. To get everything. To take everything!"

"Why? Why would they do that?"

"They think . . ."

Mom looked puzzled. She cocked her head farther to the side as if listening to a faint whisper.

"They think that, uh, this is their time. And that we, all of us, we are not real. They think we aren't real!"

She looked at me then, eyes wide. Alarmed.

I was up immediately, holding her shoulders. "It's all right, Mom. It's okay right now. It's okay."

I held her until her breathing quieted. My arms cramped, but I kept holding her until, after a while, she dozed off.

I kept physically motionless, but I was anything but calm. Why *four thousand* years ago? Why that number? What did that mean, *this is their time?*

Over the next several days, Mom stayed stable. We didn't have any more outbreaks of insanity. She didn't mention the Lizard People again, and I sure didn't ask. She began to put on a little weight. She needed it. Betty Lou joked that it was the Mander Board and Care, Ben Mander, proprietor. But it was no joke. It was true.

Once in a while I fished in the late afternoon while Mom napped. I loved the quiet, just the sound of the moving water. I loved the feel of the current pushing against my legs, and how my body would begin to automatically keep its balance against that pressure when I waded over slippery rocks. And I loved the rhythm of the casting. Back, forth, stop the rod, and the line would shoot out. Thoughts left me, and I was free.

Three or four times I dropped by Marco's place, but I kept missing him.

Mom went to Manteca with Arvin on a Saturday near the end of February, almost a month to the day after her reptile scene at my school. Saying good-bye to her was awful. She tried to smile and cried instead. I hugged her.

"Don't worry about me," she was whispering into my hair. "I'm so sorry—"

"Don't, Mom." I was trying to keep it together. "I love you. Just get better."

Arvin had finished loading the suitcases. He came up to the porch to shake my hand and take my mom's arm. "Don't worry, son," he said. "We'll take good care of your mom."

In less than a minute, they were gone.

When she left, and I was alone in the house, I found myself crying. I'm not sure I can say why. The tears came and kept coming until I was as empty as a football stadium after the crowds have gone home.

Steelhead

The next morning, loud knocking woke me. Dad? No, he'd have a key. When I opened my front door, Hubie was standing on the steps, wearing a photography vest and a cowboy hat. A cowboy hat? I rubbed my eyes. Nope. He was still there. Smiling.

"Let's go fishing," he said.

"Fishing," I said.

"You know," he said patiently, "fishing. You love it. It loves you. Line, hook, pole."

"Rod," I said, trying to get a grip. Hubie doesn't fish. His dad doesn't fish. I shuddered to think about Z's opinion of fishing. The only way Hubie would ever fish was if it was part of a complex computer game.

"Hubie, did you take a strange vitamin this morning? Did Z give you anything to help you study? What is the matter with you?"

Hubie walked past me into our living room and sat on the couch. "Hey," he said, "does something have to be the matter when a friend asks you to take him fishing? I'm ready to learn something new. Get outdoors. Go for the gusto! Be all that I can be!"

Okay, now I got it. "You think I'm losing it and that it would be *good* for me to go fishing. This is charity."

"Yeah, you look like you've been living under a bridge, but hey, charity actually comes from the ancient Greek word 'chair,' meaning 'sit,'" Hubie said in his most professorial voice. "This is the exact opposite of sitting. Sure, I think it would be good for you, or anyone, to go fishing. Even me. Plus, it's a primo day! The golden orb is glowing, the raptors are screeching, the leaves are fermenting or whatever it is they do. Time to get out, bro. Time to attack the water, terrify the salmonids, occupy our rightful place as outdoorsmen!"

The more I awakened, the better the idea actually sounded. He was right. I could see the sunshine on the trees through our windows. Late February California!

Not many rivers were open for trout fishing, and we were a little past the winter steelhead season, but maybe it would be good for me to get away from my house for a day. It had been a couple of months since I'd gone out of town for steelhead. We could be on the Trinity in a little over an hour. The smell of fresh river, a little steelhead action. Could be great! I would set Hubie up with one of my old spinning rods so I wouldn't have to surgically remove hooks from the back of his head when he tried to fly cast.

"Okay," I said, "give me fifteen minutes to do my stuff and get the gear from the garage. You sure you're up for this?"

"Does an elephant defecate in the veldt?" Hubie asked.

We parked off the road where the creek came in by Junction City. There were two other guys downstream a few hundred yards in a long straight run by the highway. I figured we'd walk across the rocks straight upstream and wade in where the river takes a ninety-degree bend. I was giving some instructions while we clomped along in our waders.

"Use the staff like a cane for stability whenever you move in the water."

"Thy rod and thy staff?" Hubie asked.

"Yeah," I said, "if you slip and fall in, you better pray, all right, cause you fill your waders with water and they'll sink you."

"Okay," Hubie said, "pay attention when I'm wading."

"Right," I said. "And I'm setting you up with a silver Castmaster. Just throw it across the river, let it sink and swing, and then retrieve it."

"I can't just leave it alone and it'll come home, wagging its tail behind it?"

"Joke if you want to, but there's a real chance you could hook up with a jumping locomotive that'll stop your heart," I told him.

"Now that sounds like fun," he said. "Does Weaverville have good EMT services?"

"You fish ahead of me, right at the bend, and let the lure swing around the turn," I told him. "I'll fish below you in the tail-out."

"Thank you for not suggesting I've already gone around the bend."

I ignored him. But I had to admit, I was having a good time out here already.

"I think you ought to use a size eight Brindle Bug," he said, surveying the water as we walked.

I was dumbfounded. I had been planning to use exactly that to start out. I held his elbow and stopped him.

"Internet," he said. He left me standing and walked the rest of the way to the bend by himself.

By the end of the afternoon, I had hooked and released three small trout. Hubie had hooked and lost what looked to be a six- or seven-pound steelie.

"I see what you mean," he said as we took off our gear at the trunk of his car. "This angling thing's got possibilities."

I agreed but I didn't say anything. I was watching a great blue heron gliding above us, neck tucked in, heading for the bend we had vacated. The air had the flat, dusty smell of granite mixed with distant fir.

I reached over and yanked Hubie's cowboy hat down over his ears. His reward for being right.

Some Mistake

Monday night I ate with the Ludlows and planned to study with Hubie. I mentioned to him that I hadn't seen Marco in the past two weeks. I said I wondered where he was, that he didn't seem to be home.

Hubie snorted, no fan of Mr. Lasalle. "My mom might know something about that," he said in a tone of voice that indicated he'd heard more than enough about the Marco matter.

I asked her before Hubie and I went downstairs to work.

"You know," she said, "I must not have understood

your story correctly. I talked with Winona, like I said I was going to. She still does shifts on the psych unit, and she said that to the best of her knowledge, no woman by that name had ever been admitted to the unit."

"No," I said, "that can't be right. Marco went in to visit her, went right inside the ward, while I was there waiting to see about Mom, the time she made a scene at school."

Mrs. Ludlow thought it over. "Well, then, I don't know what to say. Must be some mistake somewhere."

Later that evening I thought I heard a car drive up and the front door slam. I tapped Hubie to let him know I was taking a break, and went upstairs looking for Z. I found her in the kitchen, drinking some milky yogurt-type stuff straight from the bottle.

"How can you stand that taste?"

She gave me a look like I was a first grader in a philosophy class. "Women drink kefir for a number of reasons," she said, "none of which I'll discuss with you."

She was wearing a white strapless formal over Levis, red track shoes. Hair mashed down by a propeller beanie. So fun, so creative, so hot!

"Where you been?" I asked, hoping to be more like her bud than a bud of her younger brother, now that we had cemeteried together.

Again the withering look. "I've been out, Wrestlemaniac. Out. Period. Clubbing."

Clubbing? In Riverton?

"Hey, Ben, give it a rest. I got my life, you got yours. I heard your mother got eighty-sixed."

"Yeah," I said, leaning against the kitchen counter. "I couldn't keep taking care of her. Went to relatives."

"So you alone?"

"Well, your mom's really helping. You know, meals and everything."

"Yeah, but it's still pretty tough. You need a shoulder, somebody older to lean on, you know where I live." She put the yogurty stuff back in the fridge.

Shoulder to lean on. That's closer, but still not quite what I was hoping for.

Locked Unit

The next day, March first, our good stretch of weather broke. The sky had been dark during school, sheets of rain making it hard to see out the windows. I was at Hubie's and I could hear the gusts of wind bumping against their house. We were just in the middle of pork chops and cheesy macaroni with pea salad, when Mrs. Ludlow tapped her head like she had forgotten something.

"I meant to tell you sooner," she said. "Winona cleared up the confusion. A Mrs. Lasalle, to the best of her knowledge, has never been admitted to the unit, but a young man calling himself Marco has. No real ID, she said. Anyway, the reason she remembers so clearly is that he's supposed to be admitted again tomorrow."

My mouthful of peas felt like I was eating a pillow. I kept chewing, trying to get the wad in manageable shape to swallow. You accidentally kick a Scrabble board and suddenly none of the words make sense anymore. "Huh," I said.

That news sent Hubie off on a rant about how he never did trust that Marco guy, even though he had never met him.

I was glad Hubie was talking, but I didn't listen. I was hearing something else. A different story. A very different story.

I rang the buzzer in the lobby to let the nursing station know I was waiting. A grizzled middle-aged man with short, tightly curled silver-and-black hair opened the door.

"I'm here to see Marco," I told him. "I'm a friend."

"He can't have visitors tonight. Try again tomorrow." The man started to close the door.

"Why not? Is he sick?"

"Not physically, if that's what you mean."

"Why can't I see him then?"

"He currently does not have that privilege. That's all I can say."

This time he got the door all the way closed before I could ask anything else. I thought I knew what he wouldn't tell me. Once before, when Mom was really out of control, they wouldn't let her have visitors. They put her in a seclusion room, might even have strapped her down. I couldn't imagine Marco acting that way. I wondered if maybe he had tried to escape.

The next day, when I went over to the unit after school, they let me in. Marco was pacing the main hall that went the length of the corridor, rooms on either side. He didn't seem glad to see me, but he didn't try to avoid me, either. He stood looking at the floor.

"Can we talk someplace?" I asked.

"I have to stay where the staff can see me," he said, putting his hands behind him.

"What are you doing here?"

"They're keeping me here for a couple of days."

"Why?"

"They think I'm crazy."

I didn't know what to say. I thought he was crazy. I just wasn't sure.

"I told them the truth, but they didn't believe me." He looked around us.

A man and a woman behind the nursing station were watching us, but I didn't think they could hear what we were saying.

"I'm not from here," he said.

Early on, he'd told me that he and his family had just moved to this area. "Yeah," I said. "That's why the no furniture and stuff."

"I think you know what I mean," he said.

Did I? This was starting to get like my mom's world. He *was* crazy. He couldn't mean what I was thinking.

"I have to get back," he said.

He looked awful. Bags under his eyes. Face oily. His breath stank. "Back . . . " I said. It seemed like a question.

"Help me," he whispered. "Get me out of here."

My stomach slipped when he said that. Not that he was asking me to do something illegal, although I was uncomfortable about that, because the staff obviously thought that he needed to be here. No, I was getting weirded out because I didn't like what I was thinking.

He wants to go back to 4000—I mean, forward to 4000. Or he thinks he does. That's his delusion. The whole thing's been his delusion. The whole story.

But how did he know about Mom and the Lizards and my neighbors?

I got it! He was on the unit before. *He* was. He went on the unit at the same time as my mom. He was in the lobby that day when I was waiting to find out about my mom after her school visit. He was asking to be admitted because he knew he was crazy. He's bipolar! Like he told me his mom was the day I met him. The 4000 story is his crazy fantasy, and telling it to me gives him some kind of sick grandiose pleasure, like I'll think he's somebody very special. He and Mom cooked up some of this Lizard crap together!

My mind was on two different tracks. Going in opposite directions. I was getting another headache. No, the other side was saying, he wanted to get on the unit because it was part of his historical research on mental illness. He could be from the *University*. In 4000. A student from the University, using a wormhole to do his academic work.

I *was* going crazy. How could I have even thought that? Well, at least I'm in the right place!

A nurse was at my elbow. "Are you all right?"

Marco had walked all the way down the hall and was staring out the window of the staff door to the parking lot. I hadn't noticed when he walked away.

"Uh, uh, no," I said. "I mean, yes. Yeah, I was just giving Marco time to think. We're going to talk some more."

"Don't upset him," she said, "and tell him he needs to come away from the door, or he'll have to take a time-out," she added as she stepped back into the nursing station.

"I know, I know," he said, as we met halfway. He looked around again. "So, will you?"

"I can't," I said. "I have to know more. I'd have to be sure that was the right thing to do. I'd have to know what I'm doing. I'd have to know what *you're* really doing."

"Prove it?" he asked. "You want me to prove it or you won't help me get out?"

This was like his story. He was pulling *me* into his story! But it's flipped.

"They'll catch you," I said aloud. I didn't mean to say it. I didn't mean that. I meant *me*. If I run right now, the staff will catch me and they'll think I'm crazy. I've been infected. Mom got me! I was speeding up, speeding up.

"Not if we do it at night," Marco said, reaching out, touching me on the arm to bring me back.

I couldn't stay one second longer. "I have to go. I'll be back. Hang in there . . ." I was talking on my way to the door, signaling the woman at the nursing station, trying not to jog, trying not to be conspicuous. By the time I got to the parking lot, my shirt was soaked through.

I started the car. I was driving. Don't get a ticket, I was telling myself, don't get caught. I was trying to remember how to chill out. Lighten up. Easy. Easy. Over and over again, like a mantra, until I got to his house.

Up to the front door. Knocking. Knocking.

I tried the knob. Unlocked. I knew it would be. But I didn't want it to be. I wanted one of his parents to come to the door. I wanted somebody to be home. I wanted televisions and recliners and coffee tables and diddly little knickknacks. But it was empty, just like the last time I'd been there. Marco's room was exactly the same. Sleeping bag on top of the bed. No, it wasn't the same. The star posters were gone. The walls were bare.

I walked out the front door. I wanted to go to Hubie's. I did not want to be walking around the side of the house. I did not want to be looking for that oak tree. I did not want to see it way back at the end of the yard. I argued with myself until I was close enough to touch the branches.

There was something funny about the way this tree filtered light. The whole thing kind of shimmered. It was late in the day, so it was probably the angle of the sun. It could be spider mites with their shiny, glinty little webs, leaf to leaf, branch to branch. It could have been heat waves, but it really wasn't that hot.

I stood there another minute. And then another. I wasn't ready. Was I such a coward? I just wasn't ready. Yet.

I went to Hubie's instead.

Z was in the living room watching some fashion reality show. Nobody else seemed to be home yet. I sat beside her but she didn't look over.

"Hey," I said.

"Hube's still at work," she said, glued to the tube.

Hubie called it work, but I knew that messing around with computers was like play for him. Do that and still get paid. A pretty good gig.

I could feel her tensing to get up. I wanted to tell her about Marco, about 4000. About the empty house. I wanted her take on the whole thing. She looked like she had been around some pretty strange places. I mean, not at this moment. Today, her hair was flat to her head, just washed. Gray sweats, beat-up rubber sandals. Ears red where studs and hoops were being given a rest.

"Z, you said to tell you . . . if it got any stranger?" I cleared my throat to get some more strength in my voice.

Z turned toward me. The look on her face said this probably wasn't a good day for this talk.

I plunged on. "Have you ever had a friend go crazy on you?" *How far was I going to take this?*

"Besides you?" she asked. "Lately, Ben, you been looking really scruffy, eyes red like you're either strung out or not sleeping. Get straight with me, or it's private time. You know? Home alone? Solitude?"

"Hey, you said if I needed a shoulder."

"To lean on," she said. "Not to carry you around. You're getting screwed up and you're lying to me about something. I can feel it."

"What if somebody you knew was really from the future, but everybody else thought he was crazy?"

"Is this *you* we're talking about?" she asked, cocking her head as if getting the right angle would allow her to see right through me.

"No, it's not me," I said. "It's a guy who may have been spying on me."

"Okay, I'm gone," she said, rising. *"Namasté."*

She split while I was still trying to translate.

Slick

The next afternoon when I pushed the unit buzzer, the older guy with the kinked salt-and-pepper hair was working again.

"I'm here to visit Marco," I told him.

"No one here by that name," he said.

"What do you mean?" I thought I knew, but I wanted to hear him say it.

"I think you know. We're all worried." He made one of those sad grins where you'd like to smile but can't, and stepped back inside.

He escaped! I was figuring it out as I walked to the car.

They can't tell me that, but they want me to talk him into coming back.

I drove straight to his house, ran up the steps, through the front door, and into his room. He wasn't there. Nothing was changed. He hadn't been there. I went to his window and looked at the oak tree. No sign of him. That didn't make sense. And then it did.

I got back in my car and drove to my house. I found him sitting on my bed in that position he uses.

"Hey," he said. If it was possible, he looked more tired, more wasted than yesterday.

"What are you doing . . . here?" He was going to tell me the truth. I'd make him.

"I couldn't really go to the other place, could I?" he said, closing his eyes and resting his chin on his chest. "The police would look there first, and they'll probably keep dropping by all night. This seemed like the logical spot."

"How'd you find my house?"

"You told me."

"No, I didn't."

"It doesn't matter. I know where you live. Maybe your mom told me."

I didn't believe him, but I couldn't prove it. "Why did you make up that story? Why did you tell me that story?"

"You asked me to."

"You know what I mean."

He looked up at me. "It's mostly true."

"No, it's not!" I yelled at him. "It's nuts! It's a lie. It's a

154

fantasy. Or worse, you're crazy and don't even realize it."

"I'm working on something," he said. "I got caught here for a while. Really, it's as simple as that."

"Stop it!" This was like trying to argue with my mother about Lizards and lightbulbs. I *know!* I *know* it doesn't do any good.

"You're not rational," I told him.

"Not entirely," he said. "That's one of the lessons we learned."

"I *said* stop it!" I yelled. I felt like choking him, and that scared me.

"Okay," he said. "Can I just sleep for a while? I have a big day ahead of me tomorrow."

"No!" I said. "No effing way! I have some questions. What about that story about your mom and the gazebo that you told me when we first met?"

"That happened earlier," he said. "In another town. Before she killed herself."

"You're such a slick liar," I was yelling at him. "I don't even know if you have a mom! Why did you ever tell me that 4000 story in the first place?"

"You asked."

"No more, Marco. No more! The truth now. Or I'm calling the police and holding you till they come."

"Well, you *did* ask. And you were the only person, the only kid I'd met in this area that I thought might understand. It, the story, was kind of my way of thinking things over, like reviewing what had happened. I was wondering what I wanted—"

"See? That's what I mean! One minute you're a guy

from 2007, like just now, and other times you say you're not from here!" I could hear how shrill my voice was.

"Look," he said, "I'm under constraints. I tried to suggest that to you. You know it would create a paradox to bring material back in time that would then alter the future. Novikov's time-travel self-consistency principle. Well, similarly, travelers also can't divulge *information* that would change the present and lead to a different future."

"That's convenient," I said. "So, you can hide any inconsistency in your story behind that shield, and nothing really ever has to make sense."

"Everything I'm telling you makes sense and you know it," he said.

"What about the police and the SUV in the Garvins' garage?" I thought I had him.

"It may not have happened yet. They'll blame you for it, you know." He arranged a pillow behind his back and slouched against the wall. Fading.

"What about the Lizard stuff, the reptile stuff?" I pressed on.

"The skin changes actually happen, or at least will continue to happen until they get their physiology readjusted. The ideas about the red stuff I got from your mom when I was with her on the unit. She was brilliant, actually. I guess I just used those details to hook you in. I knew I might need an ally at some point.

"Some of the other things," he went on, weary, humoring me, "Bellarmine and the like, I got from the black cube on my last trip. The cube extrapolates along some kind of probability matrix. The written language stuff is also true. They call it Neuglish. It's a streamlined polyglot of basic English and the most universal words and symbols from historical world languages that have stood the test of time. So to speak." He smiled. "Once they explain it, it's easy to read the writing."

The paper with the code. "We, they, we, they. You slide back and forth."

"Yeah, well, you're right. Sometimes I can't keep it straight myself. Playing these roles. I just slip."

His lids had drooped all the way closed. Like he had been trying to fight it, trying to answer my questions, but sleep was overtaking him.

I went to the kitchen and got a towel. Soaked it in cold water. It brought him around again, but it didn't startle him like you might think.

"What is this crap about portals, wormholes?" I had waited too long for these questions. He was not going to put me off.

He dried his face with the bottom of his shirt and scrunched up against the wall to sit up straighter. "Wormholes have both a space and a time component. If the time shifts, the space may move correspondingly. They're like folds in reality where different dimensions touch. Our theorists believe this portal may not stay located at the same coordinates more than another day or two. I've made my decision. I'm going back. There's nothing for me here. And I've got to go back now. Plus, I've met a girl."

"On the locked unit?"

"Sauria. The one who welcomed me back."

He reached out as if to touch me. I stepped back and he quit.

"Look, Ben"—the expression on his face was almost pleading—"if I seem unreal to you, it's because you have known me while I was right in the middle of fulfilling my destiny. I am a man of destiny, and you have been here to witness it. I will always be so grateful to you."

"Marco, this is exactly like talking to my mom. You're crazy. You need help."

"Ben, I was never from here. I've been on the move for two years. Since high school. My family has money. I had a good bank account before my dad ditched me, so that's how I can rent places, but there's nothing left for me here. There's nothing to go home to. Dad had left. Mom took herself out of the picture my senior year. She couldn't take being crazy anymore. She was the laughingstock of our community. She OD'd."

"Right!" He was so full of it!

"True. Took all her meds at once. Never woke up.

"Anyway, here, I'm an outcast. A bum. A nothing. Gradually flushing my bank account down the toilet. There, I'm famous. I'm like a scientist. When I return, I'll publish this most recent experience. I'll be a cultural historian with ties to the Venerable Ones." He was becoming more animated.

"Marco, that's grandiose bullshit. You're going to just keep running away until something awful happens. If you treat this thing now, this craziness—"

"Hey," he said. "Don't you wonder why else I told you the story?"

I wasn't sure what he meant. "Didn't you just tell me?" I asked him. "Or was our conversation here just one more lie?"

"I wanted to show you there *is* hope to cure mental illness," he said, weary again, shaking his head. "You could even be the one who makes the next neurological breakthrough. With the ideas I've shared, you may put this century farther on the path to healing in the future. Don't you think you understand what people with mental illness are up against?"

"Is there anything I could say to get you to face reality?" I was up in his face. "To get you to come with me back to the unit without a fight?"

"Look," he said, "how could I have known about the Garvins' keys?"

"Snooping?" I said. "Working for them?"

"Okay," he said. "When I'm gone, just ask them if they ever knew a guy named Lasalle."

"You could have given them a different name!"

"Come on, Ben! The simpler explanation is that I'm you. Just shifted in time. I'm really just like you!"

"I'm not like you! I'm not like you! You're crazy! I'm not crazy!"

Now I was the one who was exhausted. See where it gets you. Argue with someone when they're psychotic. They don't play by the rules.

"Marco, we don't even look alike!" Stupid! I didn't want to keep talking this crap.

"Occam's razor," he said. "You've heard of it, haven't you? With two equally predictive theories, choose the simpler? I'm going back and forth in time! Either that, or you're crazy, too."

"I'm not going to argue with you any more." My voice was so loud!

"Tomorrow, you're turning yourself in," I said. My arms felt heavy, like I'd been in a wrestling match. I was bone-marrow tired, like you get when an opponent's been riding you for two minutes and you can't get up off the mat.

Not Too Close

When I awoke around dawn, he was gone.

I washed my face and scrounged in the kitchen for a snack. I found some grapes that weren't all moldy and some Triscuits. I was hungry for some cereal but the box was empty. I didn't have to dress since I was still wearing yesterday's clothes. I wasn't in a rush. I thought I knew what I would find.

His house looked broken-down, derelict. I hadn't noticed that before. The front door was standing open. The chairs in the dining room remained. The sleeping bag and his notebooks were gone.

I walked out to the oak tree. Looked around the area. I didn't see any other big oaks. I pushed branches aside and went in toward the trunk. The clothes he had been wearing were in a pile toward the back. I don't think I had expected that. But I knew it was staged. I knew he would have other clothes, stashed, because the police would have a description of him. He needed to change his appearance to travel. I knew he would move again, go someplace where people didn't know him, and there he'd continue to run his game. Continue to believe he was a special person who had a special relationship to the future. Continue the sad cycle of hospitalizations. Probably continue to find gullible strangers he could fool. Someone he could mesmerize in his special way. Bipolar. Isn't that what he called it?

I looked for the wormhole's wavy pattern, feeling like an idiot as I did. I didn't see it. Oh, maybe something weird with the light in the back corner. I stretched my hand toward it. *Not too close!* I pulled it back. I reached over my head and pulled a leaf off. Little sparkly webs. Mites. I knew there would be. Probably kill the tree sooner or later. What a story! What a bizarre, loony idea.

Maybe someday, I'd come back to this tree. Go inside. Walk all the way through, front to back. *This portal may not stay located at the same coordinates.* Maybe I'd bring Hubie or Z and have them watch. It would be like an experiment. Or not. Maybe someday after I graduated from high school, when I was accepted at the University.

I may have zoned out for a bit. I was pretty tired. It was chilly, but there was still light on the trunk and the glittery area and the pile of clothes. I picked up the vest and put it on for some warmth. As I zipped it, I knew why I hadn't left yet. If I was leery of putting my hand in the glittery area, then I guess a part of me believed Marco. Bought his story. What if there really was a 4000, like he described, and a cure for mental illness waiting to be discovered? What if I followed him and wound up learning how to cure mental illness back here? Mom and thousands, maybe millions, like her would be free! What a fantastic possibility!

It was noisier. Were there railroad tracks nearby? I couldn't remember. What if this tree really was a dense hologram? Could you turn up the light or sound from some master control? I looked up. Nope. Solid. I couldn't see the sky.

I tried to remember how Marco sat. So calm, so together. Like a meditation guy. I closed my eyes and I could see him again, practically reach out and touch him. And I could see the year 4000, what the buildings must have looked like. If I could get people to understand what Marco had told me . . . if Marco was right, and his work was actually the beginning of a real cure for mental illness here in 2007, I would be like the guy that discovered Marco. What if years from now, this oak tree was on a dollar bill? Or there were statues and everything! Or even a hospital—the Mander-Lasalle Clinic!

I'd start by getting Z and Hubie to understand. I'd tell them the whole thing start to finish, and we'd all be famous.

I got to my feet. I needed to tell this story right away before I forgot a single word.

Are You High?

I was driving too fast. I knew it. The last thing I needed right now was to get stopped by the police. Not now. Not when I had so much to say. So much to tell. So much to give!

A traffic officer would never understand about Marco and 4000 and this whole breakthrough idea. The police might know I knew Marco. They could think I helped him escape. They might know all about Mom and even believe I'm crazy, too.

I don't know why I'm so revved up. I'm not afraid. Am I? This is just so important! I want people to know what I know.

I probably should stop for a minute and focus. I'm getting kind of dizzy, breathing too hard. You can't keep a secret like this. Not something that will actually change the world. Make thousands of people well. Turn science on its nose. I mean, it's not like I have the answers, but I know the direction to go in. I'm the only one who really knew Marco.

Z will help me get a grip. She'll listen to me and help me figure out what to do next.

"I may have been wrong! It might not be just bugs and webs. There could be a wormhole! Like a portal, a connection to another dimension. I mean, I didn't reach my hand in or anything, but we can do that later."

"Whoa, Ben, you're going a little too fast for me."

Ben. Z hardly ever called me by my regular name.

Z was sitting on her porch steps in a band tunic and short skirt over tights. A lot of dark makeup around her eyes.

I was pacing in front of her, trying to explain what had been happening. I knew she would understand.

"Okay," I said, "sure. Well, he's gone. I knew he would be."

"Who? Who's gone?"

Z didn't seem to be able to think fast enough to follow me. Her eyes were green. Or olive. I needed to be closer to make sure. *Focus!*

I tried to slow down. "Marco. The guy I told you about. The guy from the year 4000. I mean, that's the story he told."

"You said something about him to Hube and Mom, but you didn't talk much to me," Z said, biting her lip. She was so patient with me. That's one of the thousand things I love about her.

"Yeah. Okay. I met him in the psych hospital."

"*You* were in the psychiatric hospital?"

"Yeah. Visiting. Mom and then him. And he was really nice at first, and then he got pretty strange and began telling me about the year 4000 and trying to cure mental illness."

Z shifted on the steps like maybe the concrete was making her butt cold. "Are you high?" she asked.

That kind of embarrassed me. "No. No, I'm . . . a little nervous maybe. Restless. Too much has been happening."

"I think I better get Mom," she said, looking back toward her front door.

I followed her inside and we sat in the living room. Or they did, Z and Mrs. Ludlow and Hubie, who came up from his basement hideaway to join us. He didn't like Marco, but he would be interested in more of the story. I was still too stoked to sit. It was hard to decide where to start. With Marco's access to 4000 or his meeting Monitor and Gila or the different kinds of treatment they had in the future?

"He may have been crazy, you know, but he was still brilliant," I told them. "The future is so advanced, things like Mom's illness are not even a problem. They have all these techniques, and just knowing what they called them, we could begin to—"

"Ben. Ben, don't talk quite so fast," Mrs. Ludlow interrupted. She had such a soothing voice.

I saw Hubie and Z look at each other. I checked myself. *Oops.* I had forgotten to take off Marco's vest. Forgotten to clean up.

"Maybe we ought to go to the hospital for a few minutes," Mrs. Ludlow said, "just to check things out."

Why? "You think I'm not okay?" I asked.

"Well, I think it might help us understand things a little better," Mrs. Ludlow said. "Perhaps this person Marco could be back there now. Back on the locked unit. He could clear everything up."

Wow. Good idea. I hadn't even thought of it. That's probably why Z wanted to bring her into this in the first place. Maybe that's where Marco is!

I sat in the backseat with Z. She smelled like some foreign spice. When we were almost there, I got a chill. Maybe I hadn't been sleeping enough. She reached over and held my hand! Never done that before.

I was ready to start at the beginning and tell the whole story. Maybe someone else would understand it even better than I did. For the first time since my mom went totally nuts a couple of months ago, I knew everything was going to be okay.

Wasn't it?

Let Me Get This Straight

"If he isn't back here yet, he may be soon. Really, maybe he wasn't crazy like I thought and you guys thought. If we could start studying the things they knew—"

"Slow down, please." The nurse was taking notes. She was older. I mean, really older. Sixty maybe. She was wearing normal clothes, a polo and wheat-colored jeans, and she was so skinny. Tiny, really. What was she doing working in a place like this?

"Just take a deep breath. We have plenty of time, and I want to make sure I understand."

I could feel my heart racing. *Settle down. They'll think*

you're *crazy!* "Okay," I said, making myself breathe through my nose. *Isn't that what they always told Mom to do?* "He met them in 4000. They thought he was crazy, too."

"He?"

"Marco. The guy I've been telling you about." Why couldn't she keep this straight?

"You said 'I' earlier." Her tone of voice was really patient. She was good at this.

"What do you mean?" I asked her.

"I thought you were talking about yourself," she said.

"No! No. I meant Marco Lasalle," I said. She needed to get this right. "Marco and the two scientists or doctors from 4000 got to know each other, and we could use the information they talked about."

"I see," she said.

"They couldn't get caught coming here," I explained, "because it would mess up both the present and the future."

"It would."

I know now why they hired her. She was so calm. Compassionate. "Like, if the cops found out they were from 4000, that would alter the present. Have that knowledge present in *our* world. It would create changes, paradoxes, and then their own future wouldn't be the same and . . . I'm not sure. I have to ask Hubie."

"Hubie?"

My best friend. He's a junior at Sierra High and works on—"

"What is his last name?"

"Ludlow."

"And your mother's been admitted here several times but now she's with her family in another county?"

"Yes. And the Ludlows are like my temporary guardian."

"No father?"

"Yeah, but Dad's missing in action. That's a whole other story."

"Can we have him come in?"

"No. But even if some of it's not true, we can still use the mental information. You guys can. And I can help."

"Let me see if I have this right. Your name is Ben Mander. You're seventeen years old. You're a junior at Sierra High, like Hubie."

"Yes."

"Is that the Ludlows out in the waiting area?"

"Yes. They brought me over here. Should you check if Marco's back yet?"

"Could you clarify something for me? Are you Marco or Ben right now?"

She was a really good listener, but I guess I had confused her. "Ben," I said. "I'm Ben."

"Okay, Ben," she said, giving me a warm smile. "I have an idea. Let's put questions about Marco aside for a few minutes, and I'll go check with the Ludlows about how they're doing. Would that be okay?"

"Sure. But they don't know much of what happened."

"That's all right for now." She smiled, stood up. "I think they could probably fill in some background."

"Sure."

"You can make yourself comfortable in this room," she said. "I'm going to close this door. You can rest and I'll be back in about ten minutes. Is that okay?"

"Yeah. I could probably use some more rest."

"Got it," she said. "So, I'll be right back?"

"Sure."

I could hardly wait to tell the whole story. I knew these hospital guys would get it. They'd already met Marco and my mom, and even me.

You couldn't give this kind of story to just anybody.

The Doctor Is In

They tell me I slept like a rock. I awoke to an old woman jostling me. It took me a few seconds to understand who she was and where I was.

She stood quietly by the door while I struggled to pull myself together. Marco was gone. I had thought he was a faker. A fraud, moving from town to town and spinning his pathetic lies. And then I believed he was crazy. And then I had thought maybe he was really telling the truth, and he had gone back to 4000. But the thought that shoved me off the table had nothing to do with Marco. My stomach dropped and my eyes filled.

"Am I crazy?" I asked the nice woman standing at the door. I covered my face with my hands.

I heard the woman's soft footsteps as she crossed the room and waited beside me. When I settled down, she spoke. "Would you like a snack?"

"What time is it?"

"A little after three, Friday afternoon. I can bring you some juice and a sandwich, if you want it. Either before or after, I can help you get a shower."

I looked at myself. I was still wearing Marco's vest. I couldn't stop an impulse to rummage in his pockets, looking for anything he might have left for me . . . Lint. Great.

"I'd like a shower," I told her, "and I need to wash my clothes. I don't want to put on those pajamas and slippers."

"You bet," she said. "Mrs. Ludlow came back a bit ago and left some clean things. If you want to come with me and start your shower, I'll get them ready for you."

The halls of a locked unit feel different when you've slept there. I saw two or three people wandering back and forth. One was muttering. In the nursing station, I recognized the large woman who had escorted my mother last month. The man with the curly hair was sitting at a counter, writing something in a plastic binder. I was too embarrassed to look at either of them directly or say anything. Had it finally happened? My worst fear?

The shower was a tiled stall, small, clean, no windows. The older woman handed me generic soap and shampoo and a worn white towel.

"Leave your old clothes in there on the floor," she said. "I'll bag them for you when you're done. Knock when you're ready to come out, and I'll hand in your clean things. Any questions?"

Oh, did I have questions. At that moment I was empty inside, except for rows and rows of questions.

After the shower, I walked my room, back and forth in that ten-by-twelve-foot rectangle. Ate my snack. There was another bed beside mine, but I didn't have a roommate. Yet. I didn't want to go out in the hall again. I was too ashamed. *Mom! This is how Mom felt!* I thought about what it would be like to see Mrs. Ludlow. I knew she would understand. But Hubie? What if he thought I'd gone nuts? No more guy friends. Tears came back. I walked them off. *I get it.* This is like my cell. I'm a prisoner. But it's my mind. My mind has bars around it and I can't get through them, can't get back to the real world.

The older woman looked in my door. "The doctor would like to see you in a few minutes. Is that all right?"

I nodded. Might as well get it over with.

The office was tiny, just room for a computer table, desk, and two chairs. The end windows looked out on a tree-filled courtyard. Sitting, was a tall, blunt-featured, muscular woman. Today she had on a dark blue dress with a gold medallion pinned below her shoulder.

"Dr. Bhuspodi!"

"Hello, Ben. Didn't expect to see me?"

"No, uh, I . . . you're Mom's doc." I guess I had been

expecting a nameless man, another cog in the mental health system.

"True, I am your mother's doctor, and I can assure you that whatever you say to me is completely confidential. I would never discuss your stay or your treatment with her or anyone else without your permission. However, if you would like me to remove myself from working with you, I will have Dr. Aziz from Adolescent Services work with you instead."

"No. No, I'm glad to see you. I was just thrown off for a second. I mean, it was unexpected. You know."

She smiled.

"Am I crazy?" *Am I going to be asking people that question the rest of my life?*

"Actually, that you ask that question at all is a very good indicator of mental health," she said. "Most young people, if they have a break, deny that anything is the matter. They can't examine their thoughts from a rational perspective."

"Is that what's going on? Have I had a psychotic break?"

"Well," she said, "let's examine that. Why don't you tell me what's been happening?"

As soon as I began, I started to rev up again! I took a couple of deep breaths to see if I could stay cool enough, organized enough, to give her a clear picture.

I reminded her about Mom's school episode, and her Lizard freakout at home a week or so later. I told her about Vinnie and the meth and Officer Dullborne. I told her about the Mander Board and Care and said Mom was now living with her half brother in Manteca. Throughout this part, she nodded occasionally. It seemed like she knew most of it, probably from Betty Lou's reports. *So far, so good.*

"I met Marco Lasalle right here in the hospital waiting room." I thought maybe Bhuspodi straightened up a little in her chair. "He said his mom was getting admitted, just like my mom was, the same day as Mom's school blowout.

"Marco was from out of town, possibly a little older, and when I ran into him again, here, a week or so later, he looked kind of messed up. He said he had a story he would tell me. Turns out the story was about the year 4000 and a wormhole, you know, a time portal, and looking for a cure for mental illness. He went back and forth between here and the future, using the wormhole under an oak tree in his backyard."

As I listened to myself tell this, I couldn't believe how ridiculous it sounded. Who could ever possibly believe it? I glanced at Dr. Bhuspodi to see whether she was incredulous. Nope. Quiet. Placid even. Just listening.

"I didn't believe him. I didn't. I thought he was crazy. I just got wrapped up in his story. It had details he couldn't possibly have known about my mother's ideas and my life, who I worked for and stuff. And when he told this story, he was like a Buddha. Like in meditation. Serene. But on the outside, he was getting more and more scuzzy. You know, dirty, bad breath. And he didn't have any furniture." *Slow down.* "4000 was so advanced! They—"

"What if you've been deceived?" she asked, leaning back in her chair.

"You mean Marco? I mean, sure I—"

"What if someone convinced you of things that aren't true? That aren't possible?"

"You're wrong! He . . . You mean 4000? I know. It seems impossible, but it's beautiful there. People don't have to fight anymore. They've got things figured out and they . . . Mom . . . Mom could be well and I wouldn't be so . . ." I didn't want to cry and weaken my argument. I wiped my nose on my arm and she handed me a box of Kleenex.

She waited while my breathing settled.

"Has anyone but you ever seen Marco Lasalle?"

What! "What? What do you mean?" Scrambling. "You have! The hospital has!"

Dr. Bhuspodi was now writing from time to time in a medium-size spiral notebook.

"Lasalle. Marco Lasalle." How could I be any clearer?

"And if I told you that no one named Lasalle has been evaluated on this unit in the past six months?" she asked.

"I saw him here! I visited him here twice. I know the curly-haired man. I mean, I don't know him, but I've talked to him. He'll tell you."

"I spoke to him. He said he's seen you at the unit two times lately. That each time you were upset, and that the last time you practically ran out of here."

"No," I said. My voice was too loud. "I was visiting Marco."

"Could that have been the day you were pacing the

front hall and the nursing staff asked you to stay away from the door at the end?"

I realized I had been standing in front of her desk this whole time. I sat. "Marco," I said. "They asked Marco to stay away from the door."

"Have you ever experienced stressful times in your life when you, what should we say, dissociate and don't recall what you have done for a few hours or a day or so?"

"Not that I remember," I said, realizing how foolish that sounded.

"Does the name Overland mean anything to you?"

"Like cross-country? Like no roads? Bushwhacking?"

"I don't mean the word, I mean the name."

"Uh, that trail? That pioneer thing? Or you mean some jeep or something?"

"No, like Mark Overland. Do you know a Mark Overland?"

"No. Why?"

"Because staff said you talked with him a couple of times."

"You're saying that was Marco?"

"Ben, I have no idea who your Marco Lasalle is. And I can't talk to you about Mark Overland. I'm just asking you questions to better understand what you're telling me."

"Are you saying Marco Lasalle was really named Mark Overland?"

"I don't know. I don't know who Marco Lasalle is," she said. "It could be just a name someone used with you. Has anyone else you know seen Marco Lasalle?"

I shouldn't have eaten the sandwich. It wasn't sitting well. "I don't know," I said. "I mean, other than you all. Nobody I know, I guess."

"What if Marco Lasalle isn't real?"

"He *is* real!" I looked for a wastebasket in case I had to heave. "I came in wearing his vest."

"Hubie Ludlow told his mother he thought that could have been yours. The vest. He believes he's seen you wearing it or something like it during the last year."

"Wait a minute. Wait a minute, please." I couldn't look at Dr. Bhuspodi. Why would Hubie lie? He hated Marco. He was jealous of my friendship with Marco!

"What if Hubie's lying?" I looked up for Bhuspodi's reaction. I thought I could detect just a tinge of what . . . sadness?

"You think Hubie Ludlow is lying about your clothing?"

"He was jealous! Jealous of me and Marco. He was worried. Worried that Marco was going to drag me down with him."

Dr. Bhuspodi was silent.

2027

Ben Mander. Dr. Ben Mander. The only wrestler I ever knew personally. I heard him speak today at the annual Frontiers in Mental Health Conference in downtown Boston. He looked great, spoke articulately about new directions in mental health treatment and recovery. I was there in my capacity as a director of Doctors Without Borders. I'm a doc now, too, and go all over the world.

Ben. Seeing him up on the dais, waiting to deliver the keynote address, took me back twenty years to his tough time junior year, with his mother and whoever that strange guy was. WWF had us all worried there for a while. He kind of went into a nosedive when he had to send his mom away. Luckily, my mom and Dr. Whatever-her-name-was put him back together.

4000. That was quite a story! Ben got fairly lost in it. None of us ever did find out what that other guy was really doing. The hospital records didn't have anybody named Lasalle. Mom's buddy Winona said Ben talked to a guy named Overland who went AWOL from the unit and never turned up. Any real info about him was protected by confidentiality.

Ben's hospital discharge plan specified that he stay with us, and that actually turned out to be a lot of fun. Once Ben got a little sleep and some decent food, he went back to being the fun, goofy fishing addict I had always liked so much. He had a "crazy" rep for the rest of the school year, and Hube was his only friend.

But Ben's life sort of normalized once he started winning wrestling matches his senior year. Before I left for California Berkeley, I made him a spandex headband that said *Madman Mander* in sparkly metallic red letters. Hube told me Ben wore that right up to the starting whistle in every match. I guess he was pretty good. He might even have won something at the state tournament.

When I came home that first Christmas break, Ben was hanging out with a senior girl who acted in all the school plays and, according to Hube, rarely wore any color but purple. Around then, they started all going places together, Ben and the girl and Hube and Sarah.

I laughed, sitting there in the audience, remembering the outfits I used to wear and thinking about the pillbox hat, forties rayon dress, and seamed nylons I had on today. Guess I haven't changed too much.

I knew from my mom that Mrs. Mander didn't return to Riverton. It seemed her half brother, Arvin, in his generosity, had expected his wife to do all the work to accommodate their new guest. After a few months taking care of Ben's mom, Arvin's wife filed for divorce.

Mrs. Mander had to go to a Manteca halfway house. I guess that's where she started making greeting cards with Hopi designs, and I heard she sent one to Ben every week, telling him she loved him.

Ben's father moved back in with Charlene and went back to selling pumps. Hube said Ben saw his dad in the stands at wrestling matches. They weren't speaking.

According to the bio in the conference program, Ben had gone on to college and majored in psychology. He wanted to fix people. He said he didn't realize till later that he was fixing himself at the same time. He got a Ph.D. in psych first, and then his medical degree, which led to specialization in psychiatry.

Ben wound up creating a foundation to study innovative treatments like neurological implants to deliver psych medication. One part of the foundation is the Norene Mander Fund, named for his mom. They raised money to endow an urban apartment/office complex where people stabilizing from mental illness live and work together with artists and professionals. Ben's groundbreaking article in *Science* magazine a couple of years ago charted a course for mental health research that will probably be followed into the next century.

I am so proud of him, of all he's accomplished so far. When he finishes his last presentation today, I'm going to go up and introduce myself. See if he still remembers ol' Z. See if he will introduce me to that good-looking bushy-haired advisor who coauthors some of his work.

35674046766177

CHASE BRANCH LIBRARY
17731 W. SEVEN MILE RD.
DETROIT, MI 48235
578-8002